LiTTLE LEGE

mini saga competition

- Not As It Seems

Edited by Steve Twelvetree

To granny + grandah
From Kieran

Disclaimer

Young Writers has maintained every effort
to publish stories that will not cause offence.

Any stories, events or activities relating to individuals
should be read as fictional pieces and not construed
as real-life character portrayal.

 Young**Writers**

First published in Great Britain in 2005 by:
Young Writers, Remus House, Coltsfoot Drive
Peterborough, PE2 9JX
Telephone: 01733 890066
Website: www.youngwriters.co.uk

SB ISBN 1 84602 283 5

Foreword

Young Writers was established in 1991, with the aim of encouraging the children and young adults of today to think and write creatively. Our latest primary school competition, 'Little Legends', posed an exciting challenge for these young authors: to write, in no more than fifty words, a story encompassing a beginning, a middle and an end. We call this the Mini Saga.

Little Legends - Not As It Seems is our latest offering from the wealth of young talent that has mastered this incredibly challenging form. With such an abundance of imagination, humour and ability evident in such a wide variety of stories, these young writers cannot fail to enthral and excite with every tale.

Contents

Bethany Howard (11)	37
Charlotte Haseldine (10)	38
Ashley Cartwright (11)	39
Katie Hall (10)	40
Ellie Gilbert (10)	41
Jenna Longdon (10)	42
Molly Vallance (10)	43
Lauren Cotterill (10)	44
Charlotte Measures (10)	45
Amy Scott (10)	46
Reece Shipman (10)	47
Hannah Richardson (10)	48
Scott Parkin (9)	49
Charlotte Thornhill (10)	50
Abbie Flavell (10)	51
Hayley Horton (9)	52
Thomas Moss (8)	53
Alex Harrison (9)	54
Arron Priest (9)	55
Yasmin Smith (8)	56
Jake Pilgrim (8)	57

Oliver Jackson (9)   79
Holly Tyler (9)   80

Downsview Primary School, Upper Norwood

Shabbir Chamadia (11)   81
Jordan Worrell (11)   82
Leanne Walton (11)   83
Paige Colley (11)   84
Christina Demetri (11)   85
Omar Foster (11)   86
Ryan Nestor (11)   87
Kayan Patel (11)   88
Jordan Kareem (11)   89
Lili Kemp (11)   90
Brandon Baynes (11)   91
Amir Osman (11)   92
Phoebe Kleanthous (11)   93
Amy Carvall (11)   94
Hannah Thompson (11)   95
Emma Maskell (11)   96
Katherine Linsley (11)   97

Gidea Park College, Romford

Jennifer Scollan (10)	117
Charles Thomson (10)	118
Ohenwa Cofie (11)	119
Stephanie Chan (10)	120
Jacob Taylor (10)	121
Shanuj Patel (10)	122
Jorden Griffiths (10)	123
Henrietta Woodward (10)	124
Abigail Hawkes (10)	125

Grimoldby Primary School, Louth

Thomas Croucher (11)	126
Samuel Woods (11)	127
Michael Winney (10)	128
Javon Howes (11)	129
Jamie Johnson (11)	130
Scarlet Haile (11)	131
Kieran Ryan (11)	132
Joshua Freeman (11)	133
George Daniel (11)	134
Joshua Twigg (10)	135

Llangyfelach CP School, Llangyfelach

Newcastle Preparatory School, Newcastle-upon-Tyne

Hugo Wood (11)	155
Harry Lobb (11)	156
Jonathan Scott (12)	157
Thomas Davison (11)	158
Alice McDonald (11)	159
Andrew Goldsborough (10)	160
Rebecca Rigby (11)	161
Adam Griffiths (12)	162
Gabriella Potter (10)	163
Jonathan Farrell (11)	164
Flossie Hunt (11)	165

Newlands Primary School, Barwell

Mathew Ekin (11)	166
Jade Armstrong (11)	167
Chamaine Geary (11)	168
Bailey Drescher (11)	169
Rosanna Chamberlain (11)	170

Charlotte Stubbs (10)   171
Michaela Orton (11)   172
Abigail Hendon (11)   173
Marie Ekin (11)   174
David Rundle (11)   175
Evan Marshalsey (11)   176
Paige Clarke (11)   177
Jake Lawrance (11)   178

Northbourne Park School, Deal
Leo Burrell (12)   179
Anna Douglas (12)   180

Offley Junior School, Sandbach
Timothy Hughes (10)   181

Pembury Primary School, Tunbridge Wells
Toby White (10)   182
Shelley Frankling (10)   183

Charlotte Davis (10)	184
Jonny Betts (9)	185
Jordan Tampsett (10)	186
Hannah Lancaster (10)	187
Daniel Angell-Payne (10)	188
Connor Fitzgerald (10)	189
Jack Panteney-Lyttle (10)	190
Leon Jones (10)	191
Kathryn Lawson-Wood (10)	192
Jessica Barter (10)	193
Bethany Lambert (10)	194
Thomas Stapleton (10)	195
Alec Fleming (10)	196
Adam Stapleton (10)	197
Oliver Sayell (9)	198
Gemma Bridges (10)	199
Mark Pease (10)	200
Amy Thorp (9)	201
Emma Bray (9)	202
Sasha Beeney (10)	203
Patrick Osmond (10)	204

Samantha Brown (9)	205
Helena Fenton (10)	206
Thomas Price (10)	207
Rebecca Luke (10)	208
Mia Palmen (10)	209
Daniel Edser (10)	210
Laura Barden	211
Natalie Webb (10)	212
Jemma Clift (10)	213
Catherine Goldsmith (10)	214
Bethany Pike (10)	215
Danielle Tolhurst (9)	216
Stuart Betts (9)	217

Ravenstone Primary School, Balham

Demi O'Donoghue (10)	218
Rhys Harford (10)	219
Jack Booker (10)	220
Daniel Alaka (10)	221
Jack Millington (10)	222
Miles Bassett (10)	223

Sulaiman Gul (10)	224
George Fowler (10)	225
Grace Scott (10)	226
Saskia Menti (10)	227
Alexander Clark (10)	228
Sabila Chilaeva	229

Rayleigh Primary School, Rayleigh

Katy Neighbour (10)	230
Alex Cottis (9)	231
Melissa Collins (10)	232
Tommy Nelson (10)	233
Alex Atherton (10)	234
Amelia Young (10)	235
Sam Baker (10)	236
Lewis Cotton (10)	237
Kate Turnbull (10)	238
Ben Higgins (10)	239
Elliot Goddard (9)	240
Sam Vorley (10)	241
Joseph John Lockwood (10)	242

Eleanor Howard (10)	243
Ella Pitt (10)	244
Hannah Smith (10)	245
Fiona Coventry (10)	246
Joe McCall (10)	247
Alex Thorn (10)	248
Rebecca Harper (10)	249
Aaron Lee (10)	250
Isabelle Andrews (10)	251
Tim Gale (10)	252
Samuel Blacklaws (10)	253
Sarah Davis (10)	254
John Cannon (10)	255
Robert Heaton (10)	256
Bethany Mason (10)	257
William Brant-Davy (9)	258

Robin Hood Junior School, Nottingham

Jordan Phillips (9)	259
Jack Townsend (10)	260
Peter Knight (9)	261

Gemma Macklam (9)	262
Callum Berridge (10)	263
Jordan Saunders (10)	264
Alice Norman (10)	265
Dean Graham (10)	266
Sophie Shacklock (9)	267
James Green (9)	268
Dean Duryea (10)	269
Chantelle Fawsitt (10)	270
Kuda Mushangi (9)	271
Leighanne Smith (9)	272
Jamie Kyle (10)	273
Hannah Reynolds (10)	274
Clare Hart (10)	275
Paige Walker (10)	276

St Francis' CE Primary School, Blackburn

Karam Kabbara (10)	277
Deanne Bolton (10)	278
Hannah Marsh (9)	279
Ryan Punch (10)	280

Harry Cooper (10)	281
Michael Smith (10)	282
Hannah Taylor (10)	283
Kauser Isa (10)	284
Nicola Hilliard (10)	285
Bethany Dean (10)	286
Rebecca Pinder-Coulter (10)	287
Lily Verity (9)	288
Connor Buller (10)	289

St Wystan's School, Derby

Richard Sommerville (10)	290
Patrick Field (10)	291
Eleanor Harrison (10)	292
Oliver Startin (10)	293
Philippa Stazicker (10)	294
Liam Rhatigan (10)	295
Hollie Strong (10)	296
Peter Bralesford (10)	297
Chloe Marshall (10)	298
David Boiling (10)	299

Staveley CE Primary School, Staveley

Jessica Marshall (10)	300
Michaela Raven (11)	301
Charlie Bell (11)	302
Elizabeth Crawford (11)	303
Tilly Adcock (11)	304
Frances Butcher (10)	305
Callum Gallop (10)	306
Andrew Higham (10)	307
Megan Holliday (11)	308
Laurie Nuttall (11)	309
Zoe Higgins (11)	310
Katy Coleman (11)	311
Christopher Moore (10)	312
Laurence Bowes (11)	313

Whitemoor CP School, Whitemoor

David-Arthur Opie (11)	314
Mckenzie Mellow (9)	315
Amy Parkin (11)	316

The Mini Sagas

Deceived

The thicket was too intimidating. It glared coldly before the pounce. She cleverly avoided it by stepping back but fell. Down she fell, until *thud!* She was back in reality. It was all a dream. Or was it? Two orange eyes stared at her from a gap in the curtains.

Salma Begum (11)
Cleves Primary School, East Ham

I'm Behind You

Serina walked home through the night. She realised she was being followed. The shadow came closer and closer but, when she arrived home, the shadow had gone! She was relieved. She opened the door and flaked on the sofa. Then, she heard a cough from behind the wooden venetian blinds!

Aisha Umar (10)
Cleves Primary School, East Ham

The Black Foot

Charlie was in the basement tidying up and she could hear creaking noises. Then she saw a black foot. So she went up to it and the door opened but it was only her little brother with her dad's shoes on. So then Charlie and him were just laughing.

Chloe Smith (9)
Codnor CE Primary School, Ripley

Untitled

There was a creak at the door. Lynsey ran to hide in the closet. She could feel a cold breeze on her face. It was the air conditioner. She heard the slam of a door, it was her parents.

Aaron Mee (10)
Codnor CE Primary School, Ripley

The Haunted Hour

Tick-tock, the clock went on. I couldn't sleep, I didn't know why. It could have been the large, deep, black shadow seeping through the light blue curtains. Dawn had just broken - I had never seen anything like it before.
'Hello,' came a voice. It was Bob the window cleaner.

Kimberley Ryde (11)
Codnor CE Primary School, Ripley

The Penalty

The grass was green. The ball was placed on the penalty spot. The goalkeeper was focused on the ball. The footballer's small heart was beating like mad. All was silent until he kicked the ball. The crowd was going wild. What a great goal! The best penalty in years!

Lacey Ludlam (11)
Codnor CE Primary School, Ripley

Frozen Peas

Carefully, slowly, gently the arm stretches out ...
more, more, more until ... straight, the claw softly
opens. One by one each finger extends out,
eventually creating a spread of bones wrapped in
podgy skin, reaching quickly to claw the coloured,
large, plastic bag enclosing the little, solid, green
... *frozen peas*.

Naomi Clare (11)
Codnor CE Primary School, Ripley

The Haunted House

I turned the telly on, I heard moaning from the bathroom. I opened the door, there was blood over the sink. I saw two zombies coming. The zombies came closer. I was trembling with fear, there were cobwebs everywhere. I went forward and the zombies went back and died.

Kieran Purdy (9)
Codnor CE Primary School, Ripley

The Fearful Night

It was a dark, wintry night, silent but dim. Creepy and spooky but, worst of all, something gruesome was lurking in the bushes. A sharp-teethed mouth appeared from the bushes. I closed my eyes then opened them. It was gone. Then ... what was it?

Thomas Saint
Codnor CE Primary School, Ripley

Eyes

The cold winter air touched the boy's skin. He was lost down an old country lane. A sharp rasping whisper moved over the road. The boy turned to see two big, mad eyes. A huge mouth appeared that was dripping in blood. It got closer, closer ... pounced, ripped his skin.

Elliott Henderson (11)
Codnor CE Primary School, Ripley

Awaiting Destiny

Destiny - death, as he lay on the belly of an empty desert of stirring sands. A blanket of black settled its grip on the horizon as he edged wearily towards the corpse-coated cave of the treacherous beast. There he lay, awaiting destiny. Suddenly, the walls of death crashed around him.

Samuel Hutsby (11)
Codnor CE Primary School, Ripley

He Is Coming!

He's getting closer, much closer now! Wait, where
am I?
'No, *nooo!*'
White, all I can see is white. There, I see it;
hairy, muscular but ... There, I see another one.
Longer hair, also longer arms. It's not as
muscular. *Boom!*
'Happy birthday Quentin!'
I knew it!

Dominic Bestwick (10)
Codnor CE Primary School, Ripley

The Zombie Revealed

It was there, crawling on the floor, killing humans. A zombie. It was getting closer and closer. I ran. The ugly, grey bloody-teethed thing. It started to growl and scream at me. There was a door straight ahead and safety. Hell's mate, his mind had gone all mad!

Scott Bonus (10)

Codnor CE Primary School, Ripley

They Were Getting Closer

They were getting closer! All I could see were massive monsters. A huge deinohyus had caught my scent. Just then, three more picked up my trail! I was trapped! I closed my eyes, but instead of sharp teeth, there were huge tongues licking me!

Jamie Gundel (10)
Codnor CE Primary School, Ripley

My Spell Went Wrong

I was making a potion when it all went wrong. One Friday night, I was making a frog potion. It turned into a devil! It looked at me with an old devil's eye. It was bright red. It changed to dust and disappeared. *Thank God!*

Jake Nightingale (10)
Codnor CE Primary School, Ripley

Spooky

One cold, windy night when Clair came home with Charlie they went and sat down. Suddenly, she heard a bang coming from the spare room, she went up. There was a shadow. It turned around ... It was her brother. What a great surprise! They had a cup of tea.

Jessica Hodgkinson (10)
Codnor CE Primary School, Ripley

Nightmare

One dark night there was a young girl called Jemma. She was really afraid of the dark. She got out of bed to go to the toilet downstairs and when she opened the door she heard something. *Bang! Bang! Bang!* Then, she heard a scream ...

Leanne Parkin (10)
Codnor CE Primary School, Ripley

Spooky House

It was a dark night in the house. Joe looked up; he could see cobwebs with flies' blood dripping down. Vicky, Joe's girlfriend started walking towards him then some sharp spears popped up out of the floor in front of her. Then Joe cried,
'No! Vicky!'
Then they both died.

Isabelle Hibbert (9)
Codnor CE Primary School, Ripley

Kay's Nightmare

Kay wandered into a haunted house. She stopped dead in her tracks. She heard a sound coming from the basement. Ghosts appeared from the basement and the walls and the floors. She did not know what to do! She ran outside, she ran into a zombie! It was a *dream*.

Joshua White (9)
Codnor CE Primary School, Ripley

The Old House

Rebecca was walking down the street. Then she saw a light. It flashed. Rebecca saw a big, bright house. It was spooky, the floorboards creaked. People started to talk. She saw a shadow appearing ... then some people jumped out and grabbed her. She screamed and ran away! She shouted!

Rachel Fretwell (8)
Codnor CE Primary School, Ripley

The Spooky House

I opened the spooky door. There was a big shiver down my spine. The ghost ate me up! *Help!* I ran out of the ghost's stomach. I was scared that I would not get to see my mum ever again.
'Wake up, wake up, wake up, lazy, old, silly Tom!'

Rebecca Saint (8)
Codnor CE Primary School, Ripley

I Want To Fly

I wish I could fly ... Suddenly, I felt myself
magically rising, diving and gliding to Paris. *Flying!*
'Time for bed!' Chesney yelled.
What's happened? I can't come down. I spent all
night under a tree branch. At dawn, I plummeted
to the ground, with a big *bang!*

Charlotte Henshaw (10)
Codnor CE Primary School, Ripley

A Spell That Goes Wrong

Bob got a new magic set for his birthday. 'Mum, I want to try one. Lemon juice, milk and water ...'
Bang!
'Ribbit!'
'Mum, Mum, oh no! I thought it was pretend. I need to change her back! Hang on! Milk, bread and butter.'
Bang!
'Mum! You're back!'

Lucy Bednall (10)
Codnor CE Primary School, Ripley

The Bad Scientist

He put the blue into the red and *bang!* The
invention had gone wrong. He was so hurt inside,
but all of a sudden, in walked a strange face. It
had a weapon. It said, 'Oh what have you gone and
done now?'
I realised it was Mum with mop!

Daniel Seal   (10)
Codnor CE Primary School, Ripley

Untitled

The pitch was green and dark. The last ball of the innings was coming up. A six was needed to win the game. He was running in, the ball was bowled, it was thrashed into the next field. The game was won - everyone was pleased!

Jonathan Woolley (11)
Codnor CE Primary School, Ripley

The European Qualifiers

Oooh! Gerrard shoots from the free kick against France. The ball is still in the air. The crowd begin to stand up. The ball hits the back of the net. The crowd go wild. What would England do without Steven Gerrard? How many goals has he scored this Euro?

George Hallahan (10)
Codnor CE Primary School, Ripley

The Witching Hour

I was driving in my car at 12.01 when I heard a bang. I thought I'd hit something. Do I get out of my car, but then ... it locked! All of a sudden I felt a tingle in my head and fainted. I woke on the bonnet. What had happened?

Josh Pilgrim (11)
Codnor CE Primary School, Ripley

The Haunted Manor

The door creaked open, the new owner stepped inside. The windows slammed shut, the little girl screamed. Lots of leaves blew in. The door slammed, they stepped into the middle. A faint black and white girl appeared, they backed away. They realised it was a photo of their little girl ...

Emily Melrose (11)
Codnor CE Primary School, Ripley

The Creature

The scaly creature rose from the greasy water.
Its webbed feet sank into the mud. The cave
where it lived was surrounded by damp,
decomposing seaweed. The room was smothered
in mould. Onnor, Rachel and Kate had all wanted
an adventure but not like this ...
Now, they're piles of bones.

Emily Thorpe (11)
Codnor CE Primary School, Ripley

The Haunted House

The door creaked open, the wind blowing in leaves around the dark room. Curtains blowing everywhere, the windows open. Walking upstairs, stairs broken and battered, darkening by the second. All the lights are broken, then something appears. It's ... a ghost! It's chasing you everywhere. What would you do? Shout, 'Help!'

Sarah Leanne Roberts (11)
Codnor CE Primary School, Ripley

Untitled

His piercing scream echoed through the silent, deserted wood. He quietly crept around the tent and saw nothing. He thought he could hear something but he wasn't sure. The boy stood still until he heard a creak. The boy tiptoed around the tent again and saw ... his mum!

Stacey Arkwright (11)
Codnor CE Primary School, Ripley

Untitled

As Anna opened the door of her house, she saw that the kitchen window was smashed! Mum and Dad were at work, her only older sister was in Greece - so who was in her house? Anna was getting worried ... somebody had been in her house!

'Hello!' shouted Grandma from upstairs.

Louise Cooper (11)
Codnor CE Primary School, Ripley

The Scare

The spooky house was empty. Everything seemed
strange. Nobody was home. Abbie crept inside.
The floorboards creaked. The door she had come
through slammed shut. She felt scared. She
heard a squeak and a creak.
'Boo!' shouted her friend.
Abbie screamed! Her friend had organised this to
scare her.

Sophie Stocks (11)
Codnor CE Primary School, Ripley

The Darkness

There was a boy who booked a taxi to see Man Utd play Arsenal, but when he got there, all the lights were off. No one was there ... All the lights started to flicker ... The lights finally came on. *'Surprise!'* What a great birthday party!

Michael Larkin (11)
Codnor CE Primary School, Ripley

Explosive Invention

The scientist muttered to himself; he was sure
his latest invention would eventually work. He
clamped the wires together. At first, nothing
happened. He laughed triumphantly. *Crash!* the
deafening explosion shook his hut. Black smoke
enveloped and suffocated him. He stood silently,
a look of frustration on his face.

Emma Justice (11)
Codnor CE Primary School, Ripley

Moonlit Forest

On a Saturday night Jimmy was watching telly and suddenly the doorbell rang. He jumped up and opened the giant steel door ... All he saw was the nothingness of the eerie, moonlit forest. He heard the howl of a wolf echoing through the night. He never stayed in alone again.

Jonathan Ludlam (11)
Codnor CE Primary School, Ripley

Untitled

It was creeping but you couldn't see it, you could hear it. *Bang!* A tree fell - you could hear it cracking. *Bang!* More trees were falling. There it was; a block-shaped animal creeping further - it was coming closer. I screamed. It kept moving closer. It pounced, I vanished.

Bethany Howard (11)
Codnor CE Primary School, Ripley

A Dark And Spooky Night

One stormy night, Sally walked down the garden path. There was a piece of paper on the door. She walked through the door. She heard creaky noises as she went in the kitchen. There were cobwebs everywhere. There were sharp knives on the floor. The door went bang. 'Argh!'

Charlotte Haseldine (10)
Codnor CE Primary School, Ripley

The Thing

It just kept coming closer and closer. I tried to get away but it kept following me. It was so horrible. I screamed but nobody heard me. I couldn't get away from it. There was nowhere to run and nowhere to hide. What was this horrible thing? *My little brother!*

Ashley Cartwright (11)
Codnor CE Primary School, Ripley

Lost

I walked into a foggy forest. I could hear owls and werewolves. I walked on. It got darker and darker. The trees were like hands grabbing me. The noises were ongoing. I ran, things grabbing me as I ran. And then I woke up in a cold sweat.

Katie Hall (10)
Codnor CE Primary School, Ripley

The Castle Of Doom

On a cold night, Katie opened the mansion door. The door slammed behind her, and she jumped. Katie went up the shattered stairs. She opened the closet door and screamed. A monster came out! She went running all around the house. She trapped herself and then she saw her mum!

Ellie Gilbert (10)
Codnor CE Primary School, Ripley

The Mansion Of Doom!

On a cold windy night, a boy named Jack went to a house in the middle of the country. He walked into the house and found a tunnel at the far end of the room. He saw skeleton heads and he ran out! Luckily his mum was waiting for him.

Jenna Longdon (10)
Codnor CE Primary School, Ripley

The Night Of A Nightmare

One dark, misty night, Charlotte was in her bed. She heard the floorboards creaking and the light was going on and off. All of a sudden, the curtain blew off as if someone had torn it off. She saw a reflection in the mirror and then it disappeared.

Bang! Crash!

Molly Vallance (10)
Codnor CE Primary School, Ripley

Surrounded

George was surrounded by black faces with horns with great big, sharp fangs. They got closer and closer. He turned and saw a passage. He ran and ran so fast he lost them. George had sweat dripping off his head because of the scare.

Lauren Cotterill   (10)
Codnor CE Primary School, Ripley

Scared

It was a dark and creepy night. I was in the woods alone and Dragster, the fierce-looking monster was asleep, snoring like mad. (Dragster is a monster crossed with a dragon). Then, he awoke. I started running and running ...
I woke up to the sound of a wolf howling.

Charlotte Measures (10)
Codnor CE Primary School, Ripley

The Dark Cottage

In a vast, dark cottage there were silky cobwebs
and crumbly, wet walls. The door was squeaky as a
mouse, and the floorboards looked like woodlice
had munched them all up ...
Round the sharp corner there was a loud bang on
the floor. It was an axe!

Amy Scott (10)
Codnor CE Primary School, Ripley

Untitled

I was walking home from a party. I came across a big house. I could not resist, I went in. The door slammed. I heard growling and I ran to the window and jumped out. It was a wolf. I kept on running but I tripped and it *got me!*

Reece Shipman (10)
Codnor CE Primary School, Ripley

In The Woods

It was a dark, misty night and Chloe was alone in the wood at 12am. She heard a creak, creak and another creak then she turned around and there was a massive black-grey hound. Its teeth were sharp blades. Its eyes were like fire.

Hannah Richardson (10)
Codnor CE Primary School, Ripley

Surrounded

Once upon a cold night, Julie was walking her dog down a dark alley. Suddenly, something jumped out at her. She ran faster and faster, her heart was thumping. She stopped. She was surrounded by loads of people with knives and guns. *Bang!* That's the last we saw of Julie.

Scott Parkin (9)
Codnor CE Primary School, Ripley

The Deadly Dream

Inside the pitch-black house, Katy woke up from her deadly sleep. 'I can hear something,' said Katy to herself. She could hear footsteps near the door ... 'There's something here!' whispered Katy. There was blood dripping. *Bang!* There it was. The door swung open ... an axe flew in the door.

Charlotte Thornhill (10)
Codnor CE Primary School, Ripley

The Match

Your knees tremble as the fierce man swings his
arm, aiming for the wickets that are placed
behind you. The ball comes as fast as a rocket.
You pull the bat back, it hits the ball ... the crowd
start cheering and jumping up and down.
You've won!

Abbie Flavell (10)
Codnor CE Primary School, Ripley

The Creepy Hands

Liam reached for the door handle. When he opened the door, a hand reached from the inside of the door. Suddenly, all the other people started shouting, 'Where's your mum and dad?' Then Liam started to panic. He ran out of the door. Then hands reached out of the door ...

Hayley Horton (9)
Codnor CE Primary School, Ripley

Haunted House

Tom went into the spooky house and turned round. There stood a dead zombie. There stood Tom, trembling with fear. 'What should I do?' trembled Tom. Then a noise came from the lounge.

'Happy Hallowe'en!' shouted Mum and Dad.

'What a great Hallowe'en party,' said Tom.

Thomas Moss (8)

Codnor CE Primary School, Ripley

3D Film

Albie stared at the TV as the ghosts hovered out of it. They came right in front of his face. Albie's breathing got faster. They circled him. He rubbed his hands down his face and felt his glasses, took them off. All ghosts disappeared. It was just a 3D story!

Alex Harrison (9)
Codnor CE Primary School, Ripley

Untitled

Sarah saw a mansion. She opened the door and a ghost touched her. The door was locked. She couldn't get out. She ran for the stairs, there was no exit, but she knew the ghosts couldn't hurt her because they were invisible and would go through her like the wind!

Arron Priest (9)
Codnor CE Primary School, Ripley

Who!

I was terrified in the scary woods on my own. The trees were whistling and foxes were creeping. I thought, *what am I doing in here?* Suddenly, I started to run. 'Argh! my leg!' A fox was nearly there! It started to tremble, I ran, *whoosh! Whoosh!* through the forest.

Yasmin Smith   (8)
Codnor CE Primary School, Ripley

Forest

I was walking through a forest. There was an old house. It was frightening. Noises coming from the house. I ran over and looked in. There was loud music. I went into the house, the music blared out. It was terrifying! It was a fantastic surprise party!

Jake Pilgrim (8)
Codnor CE Primary School, Ripley

Frightened

I was all alone in a terrifying forest. All I could hear was the rustling of the trees. I heard a noise from behind me. I started to run. I looked behind me. There was nothing there. I looked again, there still was nothing. I looked, there was Dad, Mum!

Jordan Elliott (7)
Codnor CE Primary School, Ripley

Spooky Forest

When I was in the forest, I stopped, I looked around then I ran and ran. Then, suddenly, there was something in the trees. Then I gasped. There was a sudden move. I ran, I fell over. Then a tree trunk caught me in the head and neck ...

Emily Hibbert (8)
Codnor CE Primary School, Ripley

Untitled

The ride began ... 'Argh!' the ghost shot out the picture. I just closed my eyes. The ride ended. I sighed. I really didn't want to go again. My cousin pleaded with me, 'Go on.' After the ride, I was sick and felt bubbly, watery. I begged not to go again.

Ellie Hall (8)
Codnor CE Primary School, Ripley

The Brown And Black Striped Bear

I went into the ghostly, ghastly pitch-black forest. Suddenly, a great shadow came out. It was a massive bear. A sudden shiver ran down my spine. I couldn't believe it. I'd finally met the black and brown striped bear. I took a photo of it and ran back home!

Nathan Thacker (8)
Codnor CE Primary School, Ripley

The Woods

Bethany went to the woods with her mum. While in the woods, Bethany went the wrong way. She heard creaking and began to feel terrified. Suddenly, she heard something, it was getting closer and closer.

'Boo!' It was her mum. She was terrified. They ran to a gate. *Hooray!*

Georgia Stocks (7)
Codnor CE Primary School, Ripley

The Spooky Old House

One day Molly went into the woods. When she came to the end of the woods, she found an old, spooky house. Molly ran to the door, Molly opened the door. She stepped inside. Suddenly, she fell down a hole! It was dark! She woke up - she was dreaming.

Eleanor Melrose (7)
Codnor CE Primary School, Ripley

The Wood

I go into the woods excitedly. In the woods I feel alone. All I can hear are the trees rustling in the breeze. Suddenly, I hear someone rustling the leaves on the ground. The sound is coming from the right. I hear footsteps getting louder. It is Mum and Dad!

Lucy Bennett (8)
Codnor CE Primary School, Ripley

Ghost

It was a terrifying noise. *Whooo!* There it was: *whooo!* There it was again. What was that noise? It's so scary.

'Argh!' I fell down to the ground. Suddenly I got up again and turned around. It was a soft brown, hooting owl in the dark, black woods.

Kealey Godkin (8)
Codnor CE Primary School, Ripley

Surprise

Everything was dark, not a thing in sight. Everything was silent. I tried to turn on the lights but I could not see a thing. But then, suddenly, the door burst open. I was amazed - we had a party. Then everyone went home and I was happy all day.

James Spencer (8)
Codnor CE Primary School, Ripley

The Wood

I was walking in the wood. I looked around. I saw something in the distance, it was ginormous. I ran and I ran till I was at the other side of the wood. I looked around again, all I saw was my dog. I went left, I saw my friends.

Rebecca Bradley (7)
Codnor CE Primary School, Ripley

The Spooky Woods

I was walking in the woods when I heard the trees creaking. I heard footsteps creeping. I turned round and it had disappeared. I kept on walking. I saw a bunch of bees. They tried to sting me but I hit them away and there they were, my parents!

Lance Edkins (8)
Codnor CE Primary School, Ripley

Murderer

It was a hot night in Australia. A murderer was walking down the street. The person had a gun. That person shot a window. The killer climbed in the window. The person inside was terrified. He tried to phone the police but the killer shot him. Blood was spurting out ...

Kaveney De Launay (8)
Codnor CE Primary School, Ripley

The End

It was a boiling hot summer day when suddenly, *bang!* The core exploded in the middle of the crooked street. I had to rub my eyes. It was, it was ... I couldn't believe it! It was like a humungous fountain but suddenly ... a massive crack ... it exploded! Nothing left.

Aiknaath Jain (8)
Codnor CE Primary School, Ripley

Walking Home

Mark was walking down the path and started hearing scary noises. The voices got closer and nearer. Mark started to walk, thinking there were zombies. He got faster and faster. *Bang!* It was just his friend. Or was it?

Matthew Carroll (9)
Codnor CE Primary School, Ripley

Zombie Boy

I crept into the forest. Eyes surrounded me. I ran as fast as I could. I tripped over a root, then I fell down a chute, knives stabbing me. *Bang!* A gun in my back. Dead on the floor. My death. I will avenge my death!

Kelan Flaherty (9)
Codnor CE Primary School, Ripley

The Reptile Room

'Hiss,' Andy could hear a snake. Andy started to walk around the room excitedly, then crashed into a glass box. It shattered. Then out came the incredibly deadly viper. It slithered out all over the floor. Then it happened, it struck. *'Argh!'* Andy woke up. Good, it was a dream.

Stephen Vallance   (9)
Codnor CE Primary School, Ripley

Haunted Mansion

John walked into the mansion. There was a hand dragging John back. There was a slam from the chained door. A smell of dead blood. John heard a loud laughing from the basement with lights flashing. He got close to the basement and they peeped out and said, 'Happy Hallowe'en!'

Jordan Naylor (9)
Codnor CE Primary School, Ripley

The Zombie

When Jessica and Emma stepped into the room, they sat on the bed. They heard a scraping noise from underneath. Then, Emma looked under the bed and she saw a greasy, horrible zombie and she screamed really loud.
Jessica looked and said, 'Get out!' and so he did.

Lauren Scott (9)
Codnor CE Primary School, Ripley

The Spook House

Maggi was creeping round and round in her mum's room upstairs. It was very spooky up there. There were real ghosts in Maggi's house, the floor kept moving and creaking. Then she sat down and it started to swish from side to side. Then a ghost made a big loud *bang!*

Stacey Walker (8)
Codnor CE Primary School, Ripley

The Crash Site

Mike walked up to the crash site. Suddenly the creature jumped out.
'It's an alien!' he screamed. 'It's going to eat my brains, it's talking to me!'
The alien walked closer. It was getting bigger and bigger and bigger. Who knows how big it will get?

Harry Breedon (9)
Codnor CE Primary School, Ripley

The Deadly Fire

Peter started to get scared by the fire on the other side of the room. There was a creak. The fire was getting closer and closer. There was a red eye where the spooky fire was. The fire was burning Peter. Peter woke up, he hoped it wasn't real.

Curtis Yeomans (9)
Codnor CE Primary School, Ripley

The Mysterious Ghost

Mark walked outside. He felt he was being watched but what by? Suddenly, he felt a cold draught go through his body. He turned and looked. Nobody was there, except a long row of houses. He saw someone walk by with a serious look on their face. *Bang!* He died!

Oliver Jackson (9)
Codnor CE Primary School, Ripley

Deadly Hands

Tara came home from school. She went to the
house door and heard a creak behind it. She
opened the door slightly and nothing was there.
She went to her mum's bedroom and opened the
door. She heard another creak and then she went
in and dead hands had appeared ...

Holly Tyler (9)
Codnor CE Primary School, Ripley

Hostage

As I was creeping slowly towards the door, I heard a bang. I then scooted to the lounge. I started to phone my friend Ben but it was engaged. I rushed out of the house, I saw a stranger. He was talking to me in signs. Ben was being held hostage.

Shabbir Chamadia (11)
Downsview Primary School, Upper Norwood

Traps

Jamie and I were running down a hill when we noticed a black house. We went to the door. A sign was on it which said, *Beware Of Traps!* We went inside and found a treasure chest. We opened it but something grabbed Jamie and he fell down a trap.

Jordan Worrell (11)
Downsview Primary School, Upper Norwood

The Doll

I started to back away from it. My hands were clammy, my head was swimming but I knew what I had to do.

The knife in Molly's hand was gleaming. 'Please be my friend, I was your best present, you said so.'

'No!' I cried.

'So be it,' she grinned.

Leanne Walton (11)
Downsview Primary School, Upper Norwood

The Flexible Figure

The leaves crunch. The wind blows. It is midnight.
I'm terrified because I'm stranded in the woods!
It's Friday 13th and it's pitch-black! I am still but
the leaves are crunching and I just felt a cold
shiver down my spine. Something's approaching
me; the figure is flexible.

Paige Colley (11)
Downsview Primary School, Upper Norwood

How Could I ... ?

My stomach turned. I felt my heart sink. Guilt ran through me like blasts of angry winds. I wondered why I did it. I'd betrayed my one and only best friend. I ran into the kitchen to find it. How could I forget to open the birthday present from her?

Christina Demetri (11)
Downsview Primary School, Upper Norwood

Alex And The T-Rex

Alex was scared. He had unleashed a T-rex on himself. He could smell the disgusting breath and could hear it stamping and roaring. Alex ran into a cave just large enough for him. The T-rex raced angrily to the cave and stuck his head through the opening ...

Omar Foster (11)
Downsview Primary School, Upper Norwood

The Invasion

My hands were shaking like an earthquake tremor and my legs were as weak as twigs. Everyone was screaming their heads off and panicking, but me, I was the worst. Everyone was running around like headless chickens. This was because the aliens had come to destroy the Earth.

Ryan Nestor (11)
Downsview Primary School, Upper Norwood

The End Of The World

John gave a potion to his brother to put in the fire but instead he kept it and lied and said he had put the potion in the fire. He drank the potion and turned into a big giant. He was so big he broke the house down.

Kayan Patel (11)
Downsview Primary School, Upper Norwood

Get To Bed, Now!

'In five minutes, get the car ready,' whispered
Ryan. He crept among the many corridors.
Rushing, he ransacked the building until he came
across the object that would lead to a successful
mission, his keys. Just as he was going he heard
his mother yell, 'Get to bed, *now!*'

Jordan Kareem (11)
Downsview Primary School, Upper Norwood

A Spell Gone Wrong

She tied me up, made a potion and made me drink
it but the witch's spell didn't work. It had
backfired. She was annoyed. She became angry
and made a new potion. I heard footsteps coming
up the stairs.
'Sue, it is time to get up!' It was Mum!

Lili Kemp (11)
Downsview Primary School, Upper Norwood

The Scary Cupboard

I was in a cupboard and I was getting so scared because there was an ugly, old guy with fungus on him and snot dripping down from his nose. It was so scary and I was so shocked and amazed by the tall, gory man standing in front of me.

Brandon Baynes (11)
Downsview Primary School, Upper Norwood

The Scary Beast

As I was running, the big beast attacked me. I was scared and ran to the basement and hid in the cupboard. My heart was pounding, I was also suffocating in the dark. The beast checked everywhere and crept upstairs. It was disturbing and scary.

'Wake up, it's a dream, again!'

Amir Osman (11)
Downsview Primary School, Upper Norwood

Storm

The night darkened, Katie was shaking with fear.
The kitchen door swung open, banging, crashing,
lights flickering.
'Who's there?' cried Katie.
A bolt of lightning flashed down in the park.
Windows slammed shut. Rain flooded the pond.
Toads jumped out of the long wet grass. What an
extremely terrifying storm.

Phoebe Kleanthous (11)
Downsview Primary School, Upper Norwood

The Wand In The Keyhole

'Abra mystic me,' Sarah shouted. It didn't work.
How was she going to remember the spell without
the spell book? Suddenly the door creaked open.
Sarah's stomach churned. Her heart pounded as a
long brown wand poked through the keyhole. The
door flew open. Sarah screamed with fright.
'Argh, help!'

Amy Carvall (11)
Downsview Primary School, Upper Norwood

Terror Bike Ride

My nails were gradually getting smaller as I bit them off. My teeth were chattering as if it were cold, but it was a boiling hot Sunday. The hairs on the back of my neck had risen and I was shivering. I wish I wasn't so scared of my bike.

Hannah Thompson (11)
Downsview Primary School, Upper Norwood

Accident

I thought he'd never notice. The teacher gave me one of his looks like he was going to do something awful. When the bell went, 'Luke come here,' said the teacher, 'quickly! Do you know anything about a ball through the window?'
'Yes Sir, I did it.' I felt better.

Emma Maskell (11)
Downsview Primary School, Upper Norwood

The Roller Coaster Of Horror

My stomach lurched, my legs felt like jelly, the wind whipped through my hair, my hands shook uncontrollably. I went to open my mouth as if to yell, but found I was already yelling. I couldn't hear anything as the wind screamed past as it rushed up to meet me.

Katherine Linsley (11)
Downsview Primary School, Upper Norwood

The Beast

He was running away from the beast. He couldn't even feel his legs and his neck was dry. His chest felt like flaming fire. The creature was getting closer and closer. Finally its claw caught him. He was very scared.

'Wake up, wake up! You've had a nightmare John.'

Mohammed Altaf (11)
Downsview Primary School, Upper Norwood

Just A Dream

The wind howled and swept over me like an evil hand. I shivered, the hairs standing up on the back of my neck. I sensed something coming closer, quite near now, almost touching me. I screamed, sat bolt upright in bed, seeing my mum standing over me. 'You're late for school!'

Vanessa Newman (11)
Downsview Primary School, Upper Norwood

Big Crash

As I was driving in the night, suddenly the street lights went out for about five minutes. Nobody could see anything. Then when they came back on, there was a huge spaceship standing in front of my car. Then my door opened and I knew I was going to die.

Hossein Arang (11)
Downsview Primary School, Upper Norwood

Stranded!

The boat stopped, the wind died and it suddenly went silent. The waves rose higher and the sea turned rough. There was nobody around for miles. The day was slowly ending, it was getting darker and I was all alone. I was scared and frightened. There was nothing to do!

Antonia Anderson (11)
Downsview Primary School, Upper Norwood

Untitled

In the middle of nowhere, Jack was there, he was scared and wanted to just go home. Then out of nowhere a fairy godmother appeared and she gave him three wishes. He wished to get out of there and for money and three more wishes.

Joshua Reid (11)
Downsview Primary School, Upper Norwood

Arachnophobia

The cave was in total darkness. I looked to see an exit. More darkness. I kept going. Suddenly, something landed on my back. Sweat trickled down my neck. I stopped and more landed on me. I looked up and saw that a massive spider was about to land *on me!*

Louis Austin (11)
Downsview Primary School, Upper Norwood

Lies

I froze. There was someone behind me. But who?
I spun on my heel and looked into the clear empty
space that stood before me. I carried on walking
but I could still hear the creak of the stairs. This
was where lies got me. I felt scared. *Lies, lies.*

Beth Tanner (11)
Downsview Primary School, Upper Norwood

Stranded

There I was, stranded, alone, no one there with me, or so I thought. Suddenly, from the corner of my eye, I saw something big and scary. It growled. I was scared and shaky. What was I to do? I tried to run fast but I was certain I was a goner!

Mikkia Glean-Lewis (11)
Downsview Primary School, Upper Norwood

Untitled

I slowly crept out of the house and suddenly someone started strangling me. I tried to catch my breath. My hands and legs were shaking and I could hardly walk. I had never experienced anything like that in my life. The light came on and I saw a ...

Shanice Okeke (11)
Downsview Primary School, Upper Norwood

The Forest Path

The day dawned and the wind howled. I was all alone. *Hoot, hoot.* There was a rustling of leaves, it was everywhere. it was following me, but what was it? I crept silently along the forest path, the dead leaves still crunched. Suddenly, it went black. I was taken away.

Laura Bright (10)

Downsview Primary School, Upper Norwood

Lonely Night

It was a normal night, like the others. Macara walked down the street, thinking how she would never see her brother and sister or her mother again and how she would never see the unborn baby, as she was running away from home. Sadness fell upon her. She felt lonely.

Jade Robinson (11)
Downsview Primary School, Upper Norwood

The Cliff

I had never been this terrified in my entire life. I held on to Kaley's legs with all my might. Sweat poured down my forehead as the waves crashed onto the jagged rocks below me. Slowly, Kaley's hands began to slip from the vine and we tumbled to our doom.

Sophie Miller (11)
Downsview Primary School, Upper Norwood

Untitled

The autumn mist gathered as the night was growing old. Laura was walking down Melrose Avenue at one in the morning. Laura had sneaked out to the most popular girl in school's party, Mandy Rose. As Laura slowly approached her house, she heard a very, very loud, scary noise ...

Aisha Hakeem-Habeeb (11)
Downsview Primary School, Upper Norwood

The Evil Dummy

I thrashed out at the dummy as it tried to strangle me. As I stopped this, it suddenly bit my leg and a toe! I roared in pain and terror. I could see chips of white bone surrounded with blood. Then I saw it, running towards me, holding a knife!

Meghna Bisht (11)
Downsview Primary School, Upper Norwood

Ben Goes To The Jungle

A boy called Ben lived in Spain. He went to bed
and had a dream. He dreamed he was in the jungle
and that he saw lots of animals. He was being
chased by an elephant. Then he heard his mum
shout, 'Get up! It's time to go to school.'

Thomas Perry (9)
Gidea Park College, Romford

An Alien Visits

It was three in the morning, I was so excited about my holiday to Spain, I could not sleep. I was looking out of my window when my whole garden illuminated. In my garden was a UFO. An alien came out and said, 'Come for a ride.'
I left.

Georgie Arrowsmith (10)
Gidea Park College, Romford

The Mysterious Death

Once there was a girl called Mary Mathews. One day she fainted and it seemed she was asleep. Her mother came to her later to find her dead. They took her to hospital and it seemed she had suffocated. No one ever knew how she had died ...

Rakshita Rawal (10)

Gidea Park College, Romford

Horse Riding

I went riding today on my favourite horse, Poppet. We were in the field, trotting, cantering, walking slowly. Poppet wanted her own way and galloped off. Poppet jumped over poles and that was when I fell off. The horse stayed with me until someone came. I was sore, my head hurt!

Rosanna Mashadi (10)
Gidea Park College, Romford

The Ghost Hunter

One day I was running away from the ghost hunter. She was after me because I was a ghost and she kept a cupboard of shrunken spirits. The hunter found me hiding, sniffing the smell of disembodied souls. I heard shouting, calling for me and found out I was dreaming.

Danisha Patel (10)
Gidea Park College, Romford

A Game Of Football

The whistle blows, the game begins. I kick, pass, run and shoot. I score! '*Yahoo!*' my team cries.

It's the second half, the other team equalise. I then get angry! I am determined to win the match. Once again, I blast the ball in the net. The whistle blows, we win!

Jennifer Scollan (10)
Gidea Park College, Romford

A Spy As A Teacher

Suddenly the police burst into our classroom, followed by a shocked, baffled, Mrs Lee. They led Sir out of the school. Henrietta fainted. Sir was arrested under suspicion of being a Russian spy, spying on Parliament in his spare time, using the school as cover. Mrs Lee walked out. Silence.

Charles Thomson (10)
Gidea Park College, Romford

Coma

Alex was playing in the road. The next minute he was lying on the tarmac, unconscious, bleeding, silent, with an ambulance in the road. They took him to the hospital. He was left in a coma. He lay in the critical ward for days but slipped away, silently.

Ohenwa Cofie (11)
Gidea Park Colege, Romford

The Monster I Know

There is a monster in my bedroom called Barker.
I like doing things with him and he is just like a
friend to talk to when you're lonely. My friends all
know him so I want you to know him too. Say hello
Barker. He is kind, friendly and loving.

Stephanie Chan (10)
Gidea Park College, Romford

War Against The Planets

'Watch it men!' said one of the soldiers as they
approached the crashed UFO outside Area 51.
I was one of the 12 soldiers. Taylor, Sgt Taylor.
A big grey-headed alien got out the saucer. The
thing fired a gun, a bolt hit me.
'Destroy all humans!'

Jacob Taylor (10)
Gidea Park College, Romford

The Raptors And
The Tyrannosaurus Rex

I was surrounded by raptors with their big, bold, yellow eyes looking straight at me, talking to each other by screeching. I was scared, they were just going to attack. A T-rex appeared and started fighting the raptors one by one. The T-rex killed them.
Something touched me ...

Shanuj Patel (10)
Gidea Park College, Romford

The Camel Chase

I was in a desert when I heard some camels suddenly behind me. Their feet were huge and they looked as if they were about to squash me. They were a sandy yellow and their humps were huge. They were a few inches away from me.

'Stampede!' I shouted.

Jorden Griffiths (10)
Gidea Park College, Romford

The Glittering Rocks

I was walking along the beach and then I saw them, two beautiful rocks, rocks glittering in the sunshine. The colours were amazing; bronze, gold, silver, dusty brown. I picked them up and then I got a strange feeling in my hand. The rock was burning, I dropped it, fainting ...

Henrietta Woodward (10)
Gidea Park College, Romford

The Camp Out

Timmy was camping in his back garden. Suddenly he heard a crash, a bang, the thump of a door closing. Leaves were rustling, an owl hooting, footsteps, closer, closer, closer. Still it was all so loud, yet eerily silent.

'Want any company?' asked Timmy's dad.

Timmy was so relieved.

Abigail Hawkes (10)
Gidea Park College, Romford

The Football Match

'Right then people, this is the final of the Champions League. We are Manchester United and we have to win this match!' said Fergie. 'You all know your positions but Tom you need to score some goals.'

We were just about to enter the field and then *I woke up.*

Thomas Croucher (11)
Grimoldby Primary School, Louth

Untitled

There I was on the front line, it was coming for me. My heart was pounding. I could hear it calling for me. 'Billy!' The noise stopped. It knocked down the door. There he was - I ran from him but he got me by the leg. I was doomed.

Samuel Woods (11)
Grimoldby Primary School, Louth

Creepy Noises

I'm awake in my bed, listening to the sound. I feel scared as I lie awake with all the noises around my head ...

I hide under the cover. *The sound's gone, it's gone,* I thought but then it comes back again. I go downstairs and find out it's the TV.

Michael Winney (10)
Grimoldby Primary School, Louth

One Dark Night

One night when I went to bed I could hear something calling my name. 'Tom, Tom, I'm coming to get you Tom!' I pulled my cover over me. Then the voice got louder and louder. Then it said, 'Tom, Tom, I'm coming to get you. Tom, got you Tom ...'

Javon Howes (11)
Grimoldby Primary School, Louth

Untitled

I was sitting in a room when a monster with six legs and eight eyes sprang up from the chair. It walked slowly towards me ... did it attack me? No? I saw another run across the wall. I was now surrounded.

'Hey, stop playing with your spider again!' said Mum.

Jamie Johnson (11)
Grimoldby Primary School, Louth

School

I was walking down the corridor when I heard *whoos* and *boos*. As soon as I got into the library, five ghost-like figures came towards me. I tried to dodge them but I couldn't. I was being nudged. Suddenly I awoke to find I'd fallen asleep at my desk.

Scarlet Haile (11)
Grimoldby Primary School, Louth

Fish

Kieran's rod was in the water ... he was holding onto the handle then he caught something. It was wriggling. He thought it was the general but he didn't know for sure. He pulled and pulled, then it popped out of the water. Unfortunately it was a fish in a welly!

Kieran Ryan (11)
Grimoldby Primary School, Louth

I Was Charging ...

I was charging through the country, when I came to a cliff. I lost my footing. I fell down. It was a bottomless pit, then I saw the bottom. This was the end of my life.
Bang! I awoke with toys on my head that had fallen off my shelf!

Joshua Freeman (11)
Grimoldby Primary School, Louth

Untitled

I was hiding in a dark, dark cave. I could hear the monster bellowing, 'Breakfast, I'll eat you for my breakfast!' It was tearing down my cave, bellowing as loud as thunder. It had nearly destroyed my cave.
I woke up! It was my mum pulling off my dark sheets!

George Daniel (11)
Grimoldby Primary School, Louth

Untitled

A bear crept into my bedroom. I was scared that it would bite me. It was coming closer. The bear walked round to the other side. It knocked my alarm clock off the table. It picked it up and put it back.
'Wake up!'
'Oh dear, is it you Mum?'

Joshua Twigg (10)
Grimoldby Primary School, Louth

Jack's Dream

It was coming closer, closer. I couldn't move.
Something knocked me ... I fell over, pretending
to be dead. It carried on walking. I followed it.
Bang! A gunshot had struck it ... it fell to the
floor. It was dead.
'Jack, Jack, wake up! It's eight-thirty,' shouted
Mum from outside.

James Storr (11)
Grimoldby Primary School, Louth

Untitled

It was one dark night ... I could hear the leaves blowing on the trees. I could hear the window flap, flapping ... the floorboards were creaking ... the water was dripping. Suddenly I heard someone come upstairs. I hid under my cover. I heard the footsteps coming closer ... it was Dad! *Phew!*

Lauren Farrow (11)
Grimoldby Primary School, Louth

Pain

I'm playing football and I've got the ball. I start running then, all of a sudden, a huge crowd of people charge at me ... I turn and flee but they gain ground on me then they take my legs out ... That's how much it hurts to have a broken leg!

Samuel Milson (11)
Grimoldby Primary School, Louth

Nightmare

One stormy night, George lay asleep in bed,
having nightmares about werewolves.
The werewolf crept into the room. George turned
over and the werewolf stopped dead in his tracks.
Next the werewolf opened his jaws as wide as
possible. He pounced and bit George's neck.
George was a werewolf.

George Young (11)
Grimoldby Primary School, Louth

The Mum Monster

I lay in bed, thinking what to do ... will the monster get me or will it not? I snuggle even tighter in my blankets, nearly suffocating myself. It's coming, groaning and stamping! I'm getting more scared now! It opens the door. It's Mum shouting, 'You will be late for school!'

Charlotte Edwards (11)
Grimoldby Primary School, Louth

Emily's Scary Night

I was in bed and the sky was pitch-black and the stars were gleaming on my eyes. All of a sudden I felt this breathing on my cheek. Who was it? I thought, *what could it be?* It sounded like a dragon. I woke up. It was the dragon!

Emily Smith (10)
Grimoldby Primary School, Louth

The First Battle

There I stood with my sword in one hand and my shield in the other. All around me men were dying. My sword struck a man's neck. As the blood dripped off my sword, I was hit in my arm by an arrow. Then I had time to get up ...

Michael Brickwood (11)
Grimoldby Primary School, Louth

The Dragon

The brave bull charged at the sleeping dragon, its horns out in front of it with especially big spikes on top. It was aiming at the eyes so it could never see where the bull was if he woke up. The dragon woke up and killed the bull straight away.

Ceejay Liles (11)
Grimoldby Primary School, Louth

Poisonous Chocolate

One day a boy went out for a walk. He was very hungry. He walked past these old women who were selling different kinds of chocolate. He bought some for 20p. The boy unwrapped it and took a big bite. Suddenly he fell to the floor. The chocolate was poisonous.

Jennifer Ashdown (11)
Grimoldby Primary School, Louth

Frightening

I lay on my bed, scared to death. The noises, the movement. I shout for Mum, she can't hear me. I hear screaming like an animal being tortured. My dad was gone, he had disappeared. He was gone forever …
I woke up; it was only a dream. Or not?

Vicky Martin (10)
Grimoldby Primary School, Louth

Shark Attack

I was in a boat. The sea was stormy. I looked at the sea. Suddenly a fin came out of the water. I thought it was a killer whale! I was wrong. It was a great white shark. It had taken my dad, the boat and now had taken me!

Adam Manson (11)
Grimoldby Primary School, Louth

Whoops!

It's getting closer and closer. The shadow's getting worse and worse. What is it? The shadow looks like it's got prickles down its back. What is it? Who is it? Why is it in my room? It looks horrid. 'Dad, there's a monster in my room!' Whoops, it's Mum!

Charlotte Tuplin (11)
Grimoldby Primary School, Louth

The Knight

The brave knight charged at the dragon. The dragon was coming forwards. He readied his lance, he prepared his shield. The dragon opened its many-fanged mouth, fire burst forward and it roared. The horse swerved and the knight screamed as he was engulfed in flame and he fell, dead.

Jessica Lishman (10)
Grimoldby Primary School, Louth

Jet Fighter

This was it, I was going to fly a fighter jet. The RAF instructor was showing me the buttons not to press. The engines were full throttle now, I was starting to move. I was getting ready to set off. *Boom!* I had blown up. The PlayStation read, *Game over!*

Gregory Lascelles (11)
Grimoldby Primary School, Louth

Star Wars Dream

I fell asleep as quickly as ever and my usual dream began. I went through the electric doors, spying and looking for the Count. Then, suddenly, he leapt out, attacking with every move. Then he stabbed me. Next, I heard shouting. Suddenly, I woke to find Mum shouting, 'Wake up!'

Christopher Griffiths (11)
Grimoldby Primary School, Louth

The Toy Car

The car got closer and closer and closer. It was going to hit me! I moved, but the car still came closer to me! I was going to get hurt ... I told my brother not to play with his cars when I was trying to get to sleep!

Carra Smith (7)
Llangyfelach CP School, Llangyfelach

Ahhh!

I was really scared - I had caught something
hairy out of the corner of my eye. It was
terrifying! It had brown eyes, it had four legs, it
was black all over its back ...
'Oh thanks! He is a really pretty puppy.'
'Woof, woof!'

Charlotte Harries (7)
Llangyfelach CP School, Llangyfelach

Red King Dinosaur

I was terrified. When I woke he was there; the Red King Dinosaur. He is a killer, I hate him. *Oh no!* He's moving, he can smell my blood and I can hear him breathing outside my door. He's coming nearer but ... oops, it is just my favourite toy's shadow!

Claire Griffiths (7)
Llangyfelach CP School, Llangyfelach

A Silly Thought

There was a boy who copied everything I did,
went everywhere I went. He even said what I
said! It was pretty annoying so I walked away but
he still follwed me! In the end I realised I was in
a mirror shop!

Tom Clancy (7)
Llangyfelach CP School, Llangyfelach

The Fiestus

The Fiestus was sleeping when Cairo the winged horse and Troi the elf came in. Troi pointed to the treasure then started towards it. It was part snake, part dragon, part giraffe and part lion. It awoke. Troi and Cairo grabbed the pearl necklace and ran, but Troi tripped over ...

Hugo Wood (11)
Newcastle Preparatory School, Newcastle-upon-Tyne

Spiders

The tight grip around my neck ... I struggled but it was too late. I could hear the faint noises of the spiders coming towards me. I panicked, I started to move even more. The grip got tighter and tighter until it was impossible to escape. I was trapped.

Harry Lobb (11)
Newcastle Preparatory School, Newcastle-upon-Tyne

Death Of A Titan

As the sun beat down on the mound of dead
bodies, the lone survivor surveyed the land.
Suddenly, a voice was heard, 'You are victorious.'
She fell to her knees. 'Why did I not die?'
The two girls were laughing. 'That was a fun game
of 'Age of Empires'.'

Jonathan Scott (12)
Newcastle Preparatory School, Newcastle-upon-Tyne

The Nightmare

He was running, running through the chilly night air. He couldn't see but that didn't matter. All that mattered was that he could get away, away from that gigantic, horrible something creature. He ran through a jungle of strange statues. He tripped and fell into the bottomless pit of creatures.

Thomas Davison (11)
Newcastle Preparatory School, Newcastle-upon-Tyne

Streets Of Despair

Rain pouring, leaves dripping, gutters overflowing.
Dark, damp, solemn figures walking in the wet.
The expressions on their faces terrible. There
are no smiles, there is no laughter, just despair.
Long gobbled alleyways with people slumped
against crumbling walls. They beg for money as
the rich walk past ignoring them.

Alice McDonald (11)
Newcastle Preparatory School, Newcastle-upon-Tyne

Holiday!

Opening my eyes suddenly, I jumped out of bed
and exchanged my nightshirt with a neat pile of
clothes I had laid out earlier.
Around 11am, I arrived at my destination where I
was being picked up by the bus with 23 other
pupils. France here I come! *Bon voyage!*

Andrew Goldsborough (10)
Newcastle Preparatory School, Newcastle-upon-Tyne

Strange

I was walking slowly down the alleyway. I heard a dripping sound. *What is it?* I thought. I looked everywhere. Suddenly, I found it. I ran away, screaming for help, clambering and searching for home. It was a bloodthirsty creature! It made snorting noises. It was close ... it grabbed me!

Rebecca Rigby (11)
Newcastle Preparatory School, Newcastle-upon-Tyne

Spooky!

The boy hid behind the sofa. He heard creepy cackles and screams. Outside he heard eerie footsteps; *thud, thud, thud* they went. He heard a rapping on the door. His mum answered it. He tried to stop her but failed. Evil creatures stood there and they said, *'Trick or treat?'*

Adam Griffiths (12)
Newcastle Preparatory School, Newcastle-upon-Tyne

The Dark Alley Walk

My hands shook walking down the alley on this dark night. Then suddenly, a window cracked and one speck of glass came down on me, but I dodged it. I then carried on walking. I was so scared. An old man came along with a tape and rope, I screamed!

Gabriella Potter (10)
Newcastle Preparatory School, Newcastle-upon-Tyne

A Dark Story

Once there was a lighthouse with a lighthouse keeper. One day, he read a dark story about a dark house, in a dark street, in a dark city, in a dark country, on a dark planet, in a dark galaxy, in the darkest place in the history of space.

Jonathan Farrell (11)
Newcastle Preparatory School, Newcastle-upon-Tyne

Mistakes

The sphinx stared at me, a cruel smile playing across her features. One mistake and I was done for. I would become victim to those flashing, slashing claws. Suddenly, her face froze and I knew I had run out of time. Slowly, she began moving across the floor towards me ...

Flossie Hunt (11)
Newcastle Preparatory School, Newcastle-upon-Tyne

The Spell That Went Wrong

Joe woke up after a very hard day trying to do his spell. He thought, then he had it! When it was the afternoon, Joe lit the cauldron and attempted the spell. It did not work. But, all of a sudden, one spark, then two sparks, then flames ... A disaster!

Mathew Ekin (11)
Newlands Primary School, Barwell

Laughing Crazy

Hanna, the hyena, was born without a laugh. Her brother, Harry, always made fun of her. Hanna was fed up with her family. She decided to go to Little Turtle's house for tea.

Hanna's mysterious brother was spying. She lunged at him, he fell in the lake. Hannah laughed crazily!

Jade Armstrong (11)
Newlands Primary School, Barwell

The Loud Bang!

The clock struck ten. I was watching a scary movie. Suddenly, there was a loud bang from upstairs. I heard my mum scream. I sneaked upstairs and saw a figure in my mum's room. Suddenly, the figure started to come close - it was a man! He was coming for me!

Chamaine Geary (11)
Newlands Primary School, Barwell

The Devil Finger

I (Bailey) was cleaning, when a knife fell off the shelf and ... cut off my finger! The finger squirmed on the table, knocking over the fruit bowl, firing oranges across the room. It turned into a ... devil! Suddenly, it plunged its fork into my heart! Was this Heaven or Hell?

Bailey Drescher (11)
Newlands Primary School, Barwell

Dead Or Alive

Driving along the country lane, Pippa suddenly
shouted, 'Stop! Noo!' There was an almighty bang.
The car stopped instantly ... 'What was that?'
asked Jessica.
'A fox!' cried Pippa.
'Stay here, I'll go out,' said Charlie.
Charlie went out. Pippa started crying, 'How could
this happen? Is it *dead or alive?*'

Rosanna Chamberlain (11)
Newlands Primary School, Barwell

He's Alive!

We were in Egypt, alone in the desert with a pyramid on the horizon. We ran for shade. We were inside; cobwebs and dust engulfed us. I ran to the nearest room; there was a tomb belonging to Tutankhamen. But, when I looked inside, he had disappeared ... *He's alive!*

Charlotte Stubbs (10)
Newlands Primary School, Barwell

Shark Attack

As Amy swam in the unknown shark-infested water, she began to splash. Suddenly an almighty fin emerged from the deep sea. Amy started to swim for her life, but somehow the shark seemed to swim faster. As he got closer, a volcano of blood erupted from the sea!

Michaela Orton (11)
Newlands Primary School, Barwell

Someone Or Something?
You Could Be Next

My heart pounded as I ran. It was gaining on me.
By now I could feel its breath on my neck, hear
its feet skimming on the floor. The air grew thick.
It felt polluted, smelt horrific. Then I stopped.
Why? I felt dizzy, sick, then my world went black
...

Abigail Hendon (11)
Newlands Primary School, Barwell

The Secret Attack

There I stood staring at the attic door, glaring at the handle, whispering to myself, 'Be brave.' I decided to go through the attic door. Suddenly I heard this noise ... a howling dog? Then a slam. I ran to the door but it was locked!
I couldn't get out ...

Marie Ekin (11)
Newlands Primary School, Barwell

Dragon's Lair

The stench of the smoke was getting heavier. I could hear the crackling of fire. In front of me was a massive red stone. The stone started to move. I could see a head coming from in front of it. It was a dragon and I couldn't escape … !

David Rundle (11)
Newlands Primary School, Barwell

The Black Widow

The spider crawled up Pete's arm. He thought it
was an ant, but it wasn't, it was a black widow
spider. The mighty beast dug its fangs into him,
then released the venom. He only had minutes to
live ...
A couple of weeks passed and *I* was still alive ...

Evan Marshalsey (11)
Newlands Primary School, Barwell

Creepy Cave

Chloe stood at the entrance of the cave. She heard drip-drops of water splashing onto the bumpy rocks. Chloe ran towards the never-ending black hole. She got closer and closer. *Splash!* A shower of water.

'Ha, ha, ha!' Molly laughed. 'Got you this time!'

Paige Clarke (11)
Newlands Primary School, Barwell

The Nightmare

One day I had a nightmare. I dreamt I had a green, slimy bogey monster sleeping under my bed. I heard creaking noises on the floorboards. I got out of bed. I went downstairs. I got a glass of water but I heard noises outside ...

Jake Lawrance (11)
Newlands Primary School, Barwell

The Flowers

The man killed me after loading his gun, setting up in the flat, drinking a single glass of whisky, receiving the phone call, driving from Texas and then putting on his suit. The black flowers arrived at nine o'clock, Friday, twelfth June, with no signature.

Leo Burrell (12)
Northbourne Park School, Deal

Night Fright

It was a dark and stormy night. Angela lay in bed, she was shaking with fright. The door creaked, Angela pulled the covers over her head. 'Angela,' she heard in a small, high-pitched voice. 'Leave me Ghost,' she cried as her little sister crawled into bed next to her!

Anna Douglas   (12)
Northbourne Park School, Deal

My Escape

As I was walking home a car came up from behind me and stopped. A man climbed out. 'Get into the car,' he said. As he said this, I noticed he had a gun in his hand. As I got into the car, I kicked him and ran away.

Timothy Hughes (10)
Offley Junior School, Sandbach

Who?

I was not alone. It was dark, and something was moving around in my bedroom. It was carrying something flat, perfect for hitting people with, and what was that? A *knife!* Fine for a kill. It walked over towards me and said, 'Here's some brownies. You want some?'
Mum!

Toby White (10)
Pembury Primary School, Tunbridge Wells

The Noise

Asleep. Suddenly ... my door shut. 'Switch the light,' I said. Shivers went down my spine. It all went quiet. I went round the house. Nothing was there. I went upstairs. There was a knock on the door. 'Argh!' Nothing there, it was my mum. 'Hello Dear, are you alright?'

Shelley Frankling (10)
Pembury Primary School, Tunbridge Wells

The Little Witch

I woke up and I wanted water. I waved my fingers, then *whoosh!* There was water in my hands. I wanted chocolate. I waved my fingers. In the other hand was chocolate. I wanted a refill of my water. I clicked my fingers, it wasn't there. I needed to practise.

Charlotte Davis (10)
Pembury Primary School, Tunbridge Wells

The Fall

I knew something was wrong, I could feel it. I looked down. I was falling as fast as a speeding bullet now. I knew I would die instantly when I hit the floor. Suddenly, I started spinning. Then I found myself lying in bed.

Jonny Betts (9)
Pembury Primary School, Tunbridge Wells

Aliens

One day the Queen was sipping her tea. She was abducted. The SWAT team came and investigated. A beam had come through the roof and taken the Queen. The next day, the Queen was in her chair sipping more tea.
I woke up.

Jordan Tampsett (10)
Pembury Primary School, Tunbridge Wells

Small And Scary

I turned the corner, I saw it. I turned again.
There was another one! I looked forwards,
backwards, left and right. They were everywhere!
An army. Where was I supposed to go? Small and
scary, probably armed with weapons. With eight
legs they could easily defeat me.
Spiders everywhere! *Help!*

Hannah Lancaster (10)
Pembury Primary School, Tunbridge Wells

The Mummy

I was at a sleepover. I'd just been told a ghost story and I was scared. My friend and I went to sleep. I woke up to the sound of creaking. I got out of bed and walked down the corridor only to find that it was my friend's mum!

Daniel Angell-Payne (10)
Pembury Primary School, Tunbridge Wells

The Coconut Attack

One day at the summer fete, I was on the
coconut stall throwing balls at the coconuts.
Suddenly, they grew legs and started to kill
everyone. The survivors were fleeing the area.
There weren't many survivors.
After a while, the coconuts pulled out guns and
hammers and killed everyone.

Connor Fitzgerald (10)
Pembury Primary School, Tunbridge Wells

The Flies

I was climbing slowly and slowly, up and up. I kept
looking down. I could see them coming. I was
scared stiff. They were faster than they looked.
I couldn't escape. They were crawling across the
walls and windows. They were coming straight for
me. The little flies were coming!

Jack Panteney-Lyttle (10)
Pembury Primary School, Tunbridge Wells

The Creepy Sleepover

That night Cheok-Ho and I were out in a tent. I heard a noise scratching the fence. I looked outside. In the moonlight I saw a shadowy figure scrambling around the garden. I woke Cheok-Ho and said, 'What shall we do?' We went outside … It was just Dad!

Leon Jones (10)
Pembury Primary School, Tunbridge Wells

The Monster

One morning I went downstairs to find my mum
cooking breakfast. Once it was made, I ate it.
Then I went to give my dog a bone but all I found
was a maroon monster. I screamed as loud as I
could!
Suddenly I heard my mum, 'Wake up Kathryn!'

Kathryn Lawson-Wood (10)
Pembury Primary School, Tunbridge Wells

In The Jungle

One stormy night, I went for a walk in the jungle.
A shiny snake slithered out from a bush. I jumped
out of my skin! Then I heard a rustle behind the
tree. A bear jumped out from behind it! *Argh!*
I heard my mum, 'Wake up Jessica!' she said.

Jessica Barter (10)
Pembury Primary School, Tunbridge Wells

In The Woods At Night

One dark stormy day, I went to a wood with my family. I decided to go an easier way but I got lost. A spider crawled onto me. *'Argh!* I'm scared - it must be past tea! It's dark.

Argh! Who's that coming?'

'Wake up Bethany!'

'Phew!'

'Wake up!'

'Ok!'

Bethany Lambert (10)
Pembury Primary School, Tunbridge Wells

Sprouts Take Over The Fridge

One night I went for a glass of milk. I opened the
fridge. There was an army of sprouts! I dropped
my cup. It smashed everywhere. I ran upstairs,
shut the door ...
I woke up the next morning - the sprouts were
gone! Was it just a bad dream?

Thomas Stapleton (10)
Pembury Primary School, Tunbridge Wells

Pirates

'Right you! Come here or you're dead!'
'No!'
'I'm going to kill you!'
They got their swords out and fought. They
fought all around the ship. On the plank, in the
cannon room and even in the diner.
'Argh!' one yelled and he was dead!

Alec Fleming (10)
Pembury Primary School, Tunbridge Wells

Nessie The Dragon

I was working. Suddenly, everyone went hot then Nessie, the dragon, shut the window and sang his song. 'Here I am, look at me, we can fight together. Here I am, look at me, it's either now or never.'
He was green and had dark blue eyes - he was very funny.

Adam Stapleton (10)
Pembury Primary School, Tunbridge Wells

The Glowing Hand

He was laying in bed when he heard glass smashing downstairs. Slowly, he went down the stairs. He searched every room in the house. Finally, he came to the kitchen. He carefully opened the door and there it was; a glowing hand, smashing all the glasses and cabinets. He ran!

Oliver Sayell (9)
Pembury Primary School, Tunbridge Wells

The Dream

It was a rainy day and there was a huge shadowy
tree. I saw something moving. It was a monster!
It came after me and got me - it was horrible! I
did not like it. It was blue with only one eye and ...
I hear ...
'Gemma, get up now!'

Gemma Bridges (10)
Pembury Primary School, Tunbridge Wells

The Ferocious Monster

I was sitting on the sofa watching the news on TV. There was a monster destroying houses and knocking on doors. It was eating people. I heard the doorbell go. I opened it and screamed, 'Monster!' It was going to eat me! It was drooling. The stench overpowered me!

Mark Pease (10)
Pembury Primary School, Tunbridge Wells

The Bad Day

First you lose your best pair of socks and shoes.
Then you're late for school when you have a strict
teacher (not good). And then you get a whole
week's detention because you aren't in proper
uniform and for being late. Believe me, it is not
fun at all! *Argh!*

Amy Thorp (9)
Pembury Primary School, Tunbridge Wells

The Bad Dream

Hannah was waiting for her best friend at the park. Then, all of a sudden, it started raining. Then thunder and lightning. Hannah thought her friend was coming when she heard a *boom-boom* noise. Then all of a sudden, she saw a ...
'You're late for school! Wake up now Hannah!'

Emma Bray (9)
Pembury Primary School, Tunbridge Wells

The Monster

Wait, I can hear it. See, listen. *Bang, bang.* I think it's someone shooting. I wonder what it is? I look around the corner and there it is ... a monster! I scream and run away as quickly as I can. I think I am going to die, then sunlight emerges.

Sasha Beeney (10)
Pembury Primary School, Tunbridge Wells

Puff The Magic Dragon

Puff lived in a cave by the sea. He lived there so
he could see his friends.
One fine day, Puff was resting in his cave, when,
what was that? He heard a noise. Puff swooped
down and rescued the princess and they both
lived happily ever after in peace.

Patrick Osmond (10)
Pembury Primary School, Tunbridge Wells

Help!

It was a windy day and Sophie was waiting for her granny. She was getting worried. She'd never been late. Then she heard a *boom, boom, boom*. It was coming closer. A big monster came in. It opened its mouth. It had no teeth. It was her granny!

Samantha Brown (9)
Pembury Primary School, Tunbridge Wells

The Nice Yummy Dream

Look over there, it's Chocolate Land! Come on,
let's get some before it's too late! I can't help
myself. Chocolate here, chocolate there,
chocolate everywhere! Oh wow, look a new
chocolate bar. Let's get some. Oh no, someone's
coming.
'Hurry up!' called Mum. 'You'll be late!'
My chocolate evaporated.

Helena Fenton (10)
Pembury Primary School, Tunbridge Wells

Pirates

'Right you, over there! Get on that plank now and jump off!' The pirate had a patch and scruffy trousers.
I felt water hitting my face. It was freezing.
'Wake up! Wake up! You're very late for school! Come on, get out of bed!'

Thomas Price (10)
Pembury Primary School, Tunbridge Wells

The Scary Dream

I was walking in the forest hearing all different sounds. I wondered, *where's my mum?* I turned around. 'Where's my house,' I cried. I was terrified. I was freezing cold like ice. I was lying soundless, asleep, tucked up in my bed. It was all just a dream.

Rebecca Luke (10)
Pembury Primary School, Tunbridge Wells

The Monster

I was waiting to go into the room. There was screaming everywhere. I went into the room. I heard a roar as loud as thunder. A bright light shining in my face ... Heaven? The light came closer, in front of me. The light then went and I saw ... *the dentist!*

Mia Palmen (10)
Pembury Primary School, Tunbridge Wells

The Lift

When I went to bed, I had a dream. I was in a shop, on the top floor. The escalator was broken so I had to go down in the lift. So I went down and the wires snapped. I fell down and woke up ... It was a dream. *Phew!*

Daniel Edser (10)
Pembury Primary School, Tunbridge Wells

Santa

Santa's getting ready for Christmas in the freezing North Pole. Pointy-eared elves, busy as can be, working away, packing presents. Rudolph's waiting outside. They're flying high, scary. But wait, someone's tiring. The sleigh is falling. Rudolph's nose stops glowing ... because he is hungry.
Will Santa give him some carrots?

Laura Barden
Pembury Primary School, Tunbridge Wells

I'm Scared

There I was, in my bed. Too scared to get out.
A voice shouted, 'Little girl, little girl, let me in.'
I shouted, 'No! Go away!' But it stayed.
The door opened. Now I was shaking. I felt so
scared. Suddenly it shouted, 'Zoe wake up! It's
time for school!'

Natalie Webb (10)
Pembury Primary School, Tunbridge Wells

Mum

Mum goes out when I'm out. She gets my presents because my birthday is coming. She is writing invites for people to come, so I get lots of presents.
The day comes. I am shocked how many people are here. There are 100 people - I open my presents. Wow, thanks!

Jemma Clift (10)
Pembury Primary School, Tunbridge Wells

Woman In White

When I was five, a tragic thing happened. I was
asleep. A scream woke me. I rushed downstairs
and my sister was pale. She said, 'Mum's drowned.'
A year passed, I got over it. I went to the lake:
there drifted my mum, in white, over the lake!

Catherine Goldsmith (10)
Pembury Primary School, Tunbridge Wells

The Big Disaster

Whizzing round on the roundabout, closing my eyes. It was great. *Bang!* I had banged my head. I came up with a greeny-blue lump. I went to Kent and Sussex Hospital, waited for about an hour. I was really tired and all I got told was to rest!

Bethany Pike (10)
Pembury Primary School, Tunbridge Wells

The Wrong Spell

Willy the witch got a letter from her parents saying they were coming for tea. She hurried into the spell room, where she was planning to make dinner. 'Hocus, pocus.' By the time they got there, tea was ready.

'Yuck!' they said. 'You must have used salt instead of sugar!'

Danielle Tolhurst (9)
Pembury Primary School, Tunbridge Wells

The Freaky House

Coming home after school, the house was really freaky. The stairs creaked, windows rattled and the door squeaked. Then Mum slammed open the door of the lounge and shouted, 'Happy Birthday!' and gave me a present. I ripped it open. It was a Game Boy! Just what I'd always wanted!

Stuart Betts (9)
Pembury Primary School, Tunbridge Wells

Honey

There is a girl called Honey. She teaches dance. One day, the hall she taught in was flooded so they couldn't use it anymore. All of the kids were upset.

Next morning, a man came to Honey and said, 'Do you want a new dance club?'

Honey said, 'Yes please!'

Demi O'Donoghue   (10)
Ravenstone Primary School, Balham

The Medallion

The shiver of fear down my spine. My heart thumped, my throat grew tight. While I crept down the sewers, there was a boy with a medallion. Men were trying to take it. I try to save him. I get shot. I wish I had never watched that movie.

Rhys Harford (10)
Ravenstone Primary School, Balham

The Black Pearl

My hands were icy-cold and a shiver ran down my spine. I was standing on The Black Pearl. I had just been caught by pirates. My feet tingling from fear of swinging off the ship. I swung from a rope to another ship and made my escape.

Jack Booker (10)
Ravenstone Primary School, Balham

Untitled

Cold sweat slithering down my spine. I felt my veins pumping. It was time to face my doom. I switched the thing on - I had never been so scared in my life. I don't ever want to watch television again - especially 'The Tweenies'!

Daniel Alaka (10)
Ravenstone Primary School, Balham

The Fight

I was running as fast as I could and my sword
trembled, my shield shook, my armour rattled and
I scrambled away. Eodean fell. His spear shook
and we fell together but we got back up ... and I
struck the great beast down - the troll was dead!

Jack Millington (10)
Ravenstone Primary School, Balham

The Mysterious Gas

I walked along the street, when I smelt a funny smell. *Gas!* I had to hide. The gas was following me home. Funny things happened - things fell out of trees, people cleared my path. There was an awful sound and a terrible smell. Remind me never to eat beans again!

Miles Bassett (10)

Ravenstone Primary School, Balham

Water Gun

I came home and shouted, 'Anyone here?'
Splat! A sound came from the cellar. My forehead
was sweating and my body trembling. The door
opened and there stood Potter with his super
soaker X200. 'Scaredy-cat!' laughed Potter.

Sulaiman Gul (10)
Ravenstone Primary School, Balham

Untitled

It's a dark day and I stare at my hostage taker.
He stares back. Then he exclaims, 'Get his
companion!'
A few seconds later, help arrives. My friend
comes and taps my shoulder, 'You're not it!'
Then the bell rings.

George Fowler (10)
Ravenstone Primary School, Balham

The Girl Ghost

I shouted, I screamed. But still she wouldn't vanish into thin air. She just stared at me but would not budge. She had been there for a solid month. Then my mum called for tea, and just like that the ghost vanished into air! I never saw her again ...

Grace Scott (10)
Ravenstone Primary School, Balham

A Normal Walk In The Park, Or Not?

The jagged teeth grinned at me. Its bloodshot eyes stared at me. I ran as far as I could. The thing chased me. *'Run for your life!'* I screamed. Everyone stared at me. The dastardly dog had chased me again. I walked home with my head hung low, very embarrassed.

Saskia Menti (10)
Ravenstone Primary School, Balham

Fish On The Run

The snake shot after me. I could feel five teeth piercing my tail. The snake's mouth was opening and closing, the bendy teeth had almost got me in their grasp. Suddenly I collided with the wall and fainted. I woke up in my new empty fish tank - home.

Alexander Clark (10)
Ravenstone Primary School, Balham

The Dragon Dream

The dragon was coming near. I thought it was coming to eat me because it had somebody in its mouth already. I was on a hill. My hands were trembling and the sweat was coming more each second. I opened my eyes and realised it was a dream. *Argh!*

Sabila Chilaeva
Ravenstone Primary School, Balham

The Wizard

The wizard stood stirring his cauldron. He yelled,
'I will turn Alice into a slug!'
She heard from outside his cave. Alice turned.
She tripped, *'Ow!'* she shouted.
'Alice,' cried the wizard. He started to chase her.
'Argh!'
'Dinner time! Remember to put your magic set
away!' shouted Alice's mum.

Katy Neighbour   (10)
Rayleigh Primary School, Rayleigh

Haunted Walls

The darkness of the night was taking over. He'd been walking into dead ends. Then he couldn't make out where he'd come from. He'd heard voices. 'Don't run away like that again. If we stick together, we can complete this maze. Now hurry up, or we'll be stuck here forever!'

Alex Cottis (9)
Rayleigh Primary School, Rayleigh

The Film

I felt the huge claws upon my neck, I was being
strangled. Then *bang!* Terrified, I did not know
which way to look. I saw a beast. The beast had a
hairy face but not hairy hands. I stood up and
then, 'Yes, I killed him!'
It's a great film.

Melissa Collins (10)
Rayleigh Primary School, Rayleigh

Age Of The Dinosaurs

'Where am I?' asked Tommy in a frightened voice. Tommy was an explorer who had travelled many miles to reach an island full of dinosaurs. 'Oh no! It can't be a T-rex ... *Argh!'*
Tommy is found by the ...
'No! A bit more enthusiasm Tommy,' the director said loudly.

Tommy Nelson (10)
Rayleigh Primary School, Rayleigh

The Roller Coaster

I'm trembling, I fall! Terrified, my mouth goes
dry. I'm going upside down. This is so scary. I'm in
a dark, dark place. It is pitch-black. I don't know
where I'm going. I see stars shining and gloomy,
dark faces glare.
'Alex! Come off that Game Boy!'

Alex Atherton (10)
Rayleigh Primary School, Rayleigh

Untitled

She was petrified. Footsteps! She could see beady eyes everywhere. She kept searching, watching. To the cave. She could feel her pulse race. It was his lair. With fear she entered, hearing heavy breathing. She saw a blue beast sleeping. She went closer and closer.
'I was watching that Mum!'

Amelia Young (10)
Rayleigh Primary School, Rayleigh

The Daydream

It was dark. I was all alone. Suddenly, there was a roar from the distance. Sweat was dripping down my neck. The beast leapt from a tree.
'It's going to eat me! Help! *Argh!*'
'You're daydreaming. I'm going to see your parents!'
'What!'

Sam Baker **(10)**
Rayleigh Primary School, Rayleigh

Untitled

'Ha-ha!'
'Freeze.'
'Sorry officers, but you're too late.'
The time machine was activated. All of a sudden a
black hole appeared, sucking in the whole world.
'What's happened? It looks like we're in the time
of the dinosaurs. Where are the rest of the
people?'
'Stop that game!'
'Mum!'

Lewis Cotton (10)
Rayleigh Primary School, Rayleigh

Haunted House

Sweat trickled down the back of my neck. Suddenly I dropped over a cliff. I held the bar so tightly my knuckles went white. The car was being watched. Suddenly a huge wolf pounced ferociously. It slowed down. I heard screaming and it stopped. I went on the roller coaster.

Kate Turnbull (10)
Rayleigh Primary School, Rayleigh

Unknown

When we got onto the beach, we saw a man. We went to check him out. Sweat was dripping down my back. My head was going round and round. My eyes went blurred and I couldn't see anything. I rubbed my eyes, really, really hard. Nothing was there.

Ben Higgins (10)
Rayleigh Primary School, Rayleigh

Age Of The Dinosaurs

I crept behind a bush. The T-rex followed. I hid just behind it and saw a cave. I peeped through the leaves at the T-rex. As I sprinted over, the T-rex tripped me up with its tail and sprang. A wet tongue licked my nose. Benson was on my stomach.

Elliot Goddard (9)
Rayleigh Primary School, Rayleigh

Ghost

I peered into the old, derelict mansion. Voices called me into the darkness. I was reluctant to go, but the power pulled me closer!
'Come with us! Join us!' called the voices.
'No!' I screamed as a reply, but they pulled me harder! It was just a dream. I think!

Sam Vorley (10)
Rayleigh Primary School, Rayleigh

The Age Of The Dinosaurs

My weary eyes wouldn't open as I lay in bed asleep. I started to dream about dinosaurs. They made deep and high screeching noises. I woke up and there was a giant T-rex hanging over me. My brother was laughing, I lay on the floor. Slowly I started to giggle.

Joseph John Lockwood (10)
Rayleigh Primary School, Rayleigh

The Shark

He saw a dark mass circling him. The water was stinging his eyes but he daren't close them. The jaws were getting closer ... closer. He felt something cold on his shoulder. It was on him!
'Come on Jake! Out now. Stop playing!'
He stepped from the pool shivering and relieved.

Eleanor Howard (10)
Rayleigh Primary School, Rayleigh

Wizard Attack

It was a cold, blustery day. The trees whispered. She ran for her life through the terrifying forest. Her heart was pounding. The evil wizard leapt through the air and swung his mace. A scarlet jet beamed from his wand. *Zoom!* 'Stop daydreaming and pay attention!' Mrs Jones shouted strictly.

Ella Pitt (10)
Rayleigh Primary School, Rayleigh

Untitled

I'm trembling, my heart's pounding, my head's spinning. Sweat drips down my neck. Its footsteps make the floor shake. It's coming closer, closer. Its evil, beady eyes staring. Its roar like thunder, breath stinking of rotten flesh.
'Mum! It's gone off. I wanted to watch the end of the film!'

Hannah Smith (10)
Rayleigh Primary School, Rayleigh

The Beast

A beast jumped out! It followed her back into the
ship. She went into her house and slammed the
door behind her. The beast started banging on
the door rapidly ...
'You shouldn't be watching that,' said Mum turning
off the TV.
'Oh Mum, I was enjoying that film,' I said.

Fiona Coventry (10)
Rayleigh Primary School, Rayleigh

Time

Back in time, the machine worked perfectly. I
felt drowsy ...
Suddenly I awoke - 250 million years into the
past. Just then, a herd of raptors came charging
past me like rockets. I walked over to the river
and saw some amazing things ...
'Joe, get out of bed!' Mum called.

Joe McCall (10)
Rayleigh Primary School, Rayleigh

Molten Lava

A gush of lava came. The temperature rose as the lava came nearer. I started to climb down the volcano. The lava getting too near. It was on me. The pain was seriously fatal. Then I awoke to the faded sound of the radio, 'Today it will be snowy!' *'Phew!'*

Alex Thorn (10)
Rayleigh Primary School, Rayleigh

A Magic Spell That Goes Wrong

Winnie the witch was busy in the basement
making up a new spell, to stop dogs from barking.
When ... *bang!* A toad, a cat, a rabbit and five
hens came rushing into Winnie's house. They were
barking. 'I really do need to get some glasses!'
sighed Winnie.

Rebecca Harper (10)
Rayleigh Primary School, Rayleigh

The Sinking City

There was an ordinary city but not for long. The forecast predicted a massive wave. The time was coming near. Then a wave too big to describe came lunging and the city was gone.
Then came the sound, 'Stop playing and get on with your bath!'

Aaron Lee (10)
Rayleigh Primary School, Rayleigh

A Confusing Spell

A witch was trying to cast a spell, *'Ippedee Dipedee Dashosh.* No that's not right, that's the getting smaller spell!' She shrank, she became the size of an ant. Her teacher rushed into the room. There was a squelch of a shoe! But thank goodness, it was only chewing gum!

Isabelle Andrews (10)
Rayleigh Primary School, Rayleigh

The Earthquake

The man with the name of Jahad was first to feel it. His tea spilled and he burnt his hand. He then fell down the crack in the Earth. What happened no one knows, except the town was swallowed into the Earth. The town has now burnt up in the core.

Tim Gale   (10)
Rayleigh Primary School, Rayleigh

The Spell

Zap! Hooray! It's worked. My house has grown,
but it's still growing! He tried for hours but
nothing happened. He had to fly it to a field. The
teacher had to vanish it.
'So I'm homeless?' he asked.
'Of course not. Now get out of bed!' replied Mum.

Samuel Blacklaws (10)
Rayleigh Primary School, Rayleigh

The Dinosaur Egg

There I was, standing in the middle of the desert next to a dinosaur egg! I touched it. The egg cracked and a tiny, but scary head, popped out. I gasped. The little head revealed a body. It cocked its head on one side and tiptoed away.

Sarah Davis (10)
Rayleigh Primary School, Rayleigh

The Potion That Went Wrong

I created a magic potion. I dropped it on my head.
I ran to hospital because my head was a fly's
head. Everyone ran away. I thought I looked
handsome. I went home and I married a nice-
looking fly and lived a happy, long-lasting life with
that fly.

John Cannon (10)
Rayleigh Primary School, Rayleigh

Terrible Time!

Chris heard a click and knew it was ready. So he came, cursing. He steadily opened the door and what he saw was terrifying. He heard the noises stop and heard footsteps. It was what he dreaded. Dinner was ready and all was lost.

Robert Heaton (10)
Rayleigh Primary School, Rayleigh

Judy Moody Had A Bad Dream

Judy Moody was in a mood. She did not want to get up. It was a weekend, so she didn't have to get up. She started to do some drawing. Then suddenly it all went dark. Lightning struck. Judy screamed.

'Judy get up!' Judy's mum shouted, 'and that's now Judy!'

Bethany Mason (10)
Rayleigh Primary School, Rayleigh

Black Shuck

Walking along the street in Southend, I spotted a black dog. I walked over to it. It whizzed around, my heart pounded. I looked into its eyes, they were like fire! I ran as fast as I could. It ran after me! *'Help!'* My head started to spin ...

William Brant-Davy (9)
Rayleigh Primary School, Rayleigh

The Water Collector

One day in a place, an old man lived. He was poor.
he sent his wife to ask his daughter to fetch
some clear water from the river. She got
followed by a cart. She began to walk faster and
faster and soon she began to run faster home.

Jordan Phillips   (9)
Robin Hood Junior School, Nottingham

The Big Disgusting Spider

One night I saw a gigantic spider run across the
lino. It was the most vile thing you ever would see
in your life. It had eight hairy legs. It was
petrifying! It was black and hairy like the Devil.
My brother said to me, 'It was just me playing
with my toy spider!'

Jack Townsend (10)
Robin Hood Junior School, Nottingham

The Savage Monster

A man was walking in the woods. Something ran past. The monster was ready to attack … with savage claws, the monster was ripping his guts, gore and his brain with blood dripping from his claws. He was not human anymore. With a thunderous roar, he destroyed half of the world.

Peter Knight (9)
Robin Hood Junior School, Nottingham

The Snake And Jay

It was closer. It was in his bedroom. Jay stepped back. He was petrified. He quickly climbed onto his bed. I grabbed his fake sword and hit the snake. *Missed!* He ran to his toy box and hit it. Now it was dead. Then he saw his cat moving the wool.

Gemma Macklam (9)
Robin Hood Junior School, Nottingham

Cross On The Door

Morgiana had a master who stole from some thieves.

One day Morgiana came home from shopping and she saw a cross on her door. She put her bags down and she thought, *Who would have done it and why?* The answer caught her.

It was the thieves.

Callum Berridge (10)
Robin Hood Junior School, Nottingham

Troll Attack

She escaped out of her collar and saw Butler smashed into the wall. She looked around. No one was there. Suddenly a troll jumped out and almost crushed Holly to the ground! His mum popped out of the troll. His mum was the controller; it was an electric troll.

Jordan Saunders (10)
Robin Hood Junior School, Nottingham

Potion Trouble

The wizard dropped the toad into the potion and
stirred it gleefully.
'I'm sure I've got it right this time! Josh, come
here, try this.'
Josh drank the potion and collapsed on the floor.
Two minutes later Josh stood up, but he wasn't
himself ... he was a tiger!
'Whoops!'
'Roooaaar!'

Alice Norman (10)
Robin Hood Junior School, Nottingham

The Werewolf In The Living Forest

On Sunday I went to the forest to catch a
werewolf. I saw something move … It chucked an
eyeball at me … I screamed! The werewolf ran off
howling. It ripped off its face …
It was a young boy.

Dean Graham (10)
Robin Hood Junior School, Nottingham

The Wind

The wind is blowing, blowing the trees down and the twister is coming! The people are in their houses. The wind is slowing down. The twister is getting faster and faster and bigger and harder. It's raining too.

Sophie Shacklock (9)
Robin Hood Junior School, Nottingham

Invading Aliens

Troy was going into his bedroom. He went to open the window and he saw something hovering. A beam of light came down and it was sucking people up. They were petrified! They turned his TV on and it said, 'Aliens are invading the Earth.' Suddenly, aliens ruled.

James Green (9)
Robin Hood Junior School, Nottingham

Goldilocks And The Three Ugly Bears

Goldilocks was walking through the forest. She saw a house. Goldilocks sat in Daddy's, Mummy's and Baby's chairs. She ate the porridge and she was tired. She slept in every bed. She fell asleep in Baby Bear's bed. The bears saw her and Goldilocks ran and shouted, 'Sorry!'

Dean Duryea (10)
Robin Hood Junior School, Nottingham

Myths And Legends

As I walked home, I saw a cross on my door, but not on the other doors. So I put crosses on the other doors. After I did it, I moved house. So Ali Baba didn't get hurt. No one knew where we lived. So Ali Baba didn't get hurt.

Chantelle Fawsitt (10)
Robin Hood Junior School, Nottingham

The Record-Breaking Champion

It was time to try and break the speed of sound record and there were only two hours to go. I was anxious, but I knew if I didn't make it my children would remember me as a hero. Thirty minutes ... and the sonic boom exploded. I made history.

Kuda Mushangi (9)
Robin Hood Junior School, Nottingham

Three Little Pigs

Long, long ago there were three pigs. One built his house out of hay. Along came Wolf; he blew the house down. Another little pig, she built a house of sticks. Wolf blew it down. The next one made a house of bricks. Wolf couldn't blow the house down.

Leighanne Smith (9)
Robin Hood Junior School, Nottingham

Goldilocks And The Three Bears

Once upon a time there lived three bears. There was a girl called Goldilocks, she walked into the bears' house and saw all of the chairs. She ate all of the porridge and went upstairs. She went to bed. The bears came back and Goldilocks said sorry and ran away.

Jamie Kyle (10)

Robin Hood Junior School, Nottingham

The Three Pigs

One day I was walking down the road and I saw three little pigs. Me and my two friends saw them walking towards us. We saw a mirror and walked to it. They were getting closer and we realised it was only us three walking up to a mirror.

Hannah Reynolds   (10)
Robin Hood Junior School, Nottingham

Help!

I was in my bedroom sitting all alone as usual when all of a sudden my cat, Fleaball pounced off my bed. My teacher shouted, 'Lights out witches!' If you haven't guessed by now, I go to an all witches boarding school. *Help!* I need to get out of here!

Clare Hart (10)
Robin Hood Junior School, Nottingham

How Is Grandad?

With his blood pressure low, he was rushed to
hospital, lights flashing blue and red. My heart
sank. I couldn't sleep. Minutes later I asked Mum.
She drove me to hospital, Grandad was plugged in.
Hours later, nurses and doctors pushed, I
understood that sound, a suffering beep of ...
Life!

Paige Walker (10)
Robin Hood Junior School, Nottingham

Stellios And The Relic

At the stroke of midnight, the relic stumbled out of its gloomy cave onto the murky mountain. The relic's five heads twisted and turned, its eyes stared left to right as they were glowing from green to orange to fiery red. Its nose sniffing mentally for the scent of children.

Karam Kabbara (10)
St Francis' CE Primary School, Blackburn

The Minagog

The Minagog started to move closer. Its wooden feet clomped around the city, its bellowing roar echoed in the moonlight. Then, suddenly, it ran to Redland Hill and whipped its whipping tail and started munching on its earlier victim. It jumped off the hill and made a gigantic thud.

Deanne Bolton (10)
St Francis' CE Primary School, Blackburn

Arthur And The Destroyer

The massive, three-headed monster entered the island. Villagers ran into their homes to hide. But that night the Destroyer stole valuables and food and destroyed homes. One brave warrior, Arthur, was determined to kill this beast. A poisonous apple was his plot, hidden in the giant's dark, dingy cave.

Hannah Marsh (9)
St Francis' CE Primary School, Blackburn

The Killing

The house was dark, nobody was in. But then something ran across the room. She heard footsteps coming towards her. What was it, she wondered. She was terrified. It was Nogard, the beast. She had heard that he was killing people! Would it get her or would it not ...?

Ryan Punch (10)
St Francis' CE Primary School, Blackburn

Dreaming

I was going to the garage to feed my ferret Frankie. He was gone, I could see a trail of blood. I followed the trail with my heart in my mouth. In the distance I could hear someone shouting my name. 'Harry, Harry, Harry! It's time to get up!'

Harry Cooper (10)
St Francis' CE Primary School, Blackburn

Zidane And The Elder Sword

'So this is what is feels like.' Zidane slowly gripped the scabbard of the elder sword. Just then, a ferocious soldier came rushing up, sword in hand. 'Argh!' a second later he was crawling along the floor. *'Uhhh!'* Zidane was astonished - it did it automatically. On its own! Zidane glared.

Michael Smith (10)
St Francis' CE Primary School, Blackburn

The Sting Spirit

It drifted over to me. I struggled to break free!
It was too difficult. Finally, I managed to get
loose and run! I ran and ran very fast, until I
came to a dead end! I panicked and my mum woke
me up. 'Sarah, are you OK?' she said calmly.

Hannah Taylor (10)
St Francis' CE Primary School, Blackburn

Arthur And The Dragspon

Arthur got the skin of a goat, filled it with tar and brimstone and waited. The beast awoke, ate the skin of the goat. *Great!* The beast burnt with fire. It could not drink because the desert was dry, all it could do was suffer. Seconds later, the beast exploded!

Kauser Isa (10)

St Francis' CE Primary School, Blackburn

Romeo And The Dragle

Once in the ancient town of Athens, Prince Romeo
was sleeping. *'Argh!'* He awoke; a Dragle was
outside staring through the window. Romeo ran
downstairs and outside. Then jumped on top of
the Dragle and stabbed him in the neck! Athens
was saved! All thanks to Prince Romeo!

Nicola Hilliard (10)
St Francis' CE Primary School, Blackburn

Striker

'Striker,' they all shouted, running into their homes.
'The day has come,' said the king.
The massive dragon appeared out of nowhere. His whipping tail and his wings made a wailing wind. It pounced onto the ground and crawled into the palace, crashing through the princess' wall. It grabbed her!

Bethany Dean (10)
St Francis' CE Primary School, Blackburn

Basilisk

It was the Basilisk who was getting the urge to follow me, but then, all of a sudden I heard a noise and it was coming closer. When all of a sudden ... 'Wake up Becky, it's late! Come on!' It was all just a very silly, nasty, little dream.

Rebecca Pinder-Coulter (10)
St Francis' CE Primary School, Blackburn

The Stench Of The Stink Spirit

The slug-like creature slithered through the gates of the city of Lafia. The monster's terrible stench filled the city; every flower shrivelled up and died because of the stench. Mud oozed off the monster's body. It let out a monstrous cry. It was definitely a stink spirit's cry. Argh!

Lily Verity (9)
St Francis' CE Primary School, Blackburn

The Legend Beast

It was a life and death situation. I couldn't feel my bones, I was that worried. I went to the stone one little baby step every five seconds. As I finally got to the rock, I clenched the handle of the sword. But then, something jumped out at me. Argh!

Connor Buller (10)
St Francis' CE Primary School, Blackburn

The Granny With The Gun

Tim and Nick boarded the Eurostar to France and found seats next to an old lady and a man from Texas. They were detectives tracking the mad American and drug smuggling scam. The lady drew a gun, she was their target! But they were too fast for her. *Bang!*

Richard Sommerville (10)
St Wystan's School, Derby

Alien Attack

The girl watched as the shaft of light hit the ground and a strange figure emerged. She was so scared she didn't move one inch. Suddenly the house door flew open. There stood Mum. She shouted, 'Are you mad standing out in a storm?' Pulling the girl inside.

Patrick Field (10)
St Wystan's School, Derby

Going Up?

Poppy and Madeline pressed the button for the
lift and trudged inside. Poppy pushed the light
and the lift moved, but this time it moved
sideways. Suddenly it stopped. The door opened.
Where were they? Everything began to sway.
'Wake up, sleepyhead,' cried Mum shaking her,
'your food's cold.'

Eleanor Harrison (10)
St Wystan's School, Derby

Midnight Encounter

The dark shape advanced on me. Powerful claws glinting in the night. I trembled with fear. A jet-black creature with eyes like two lamps glowing in the darkness. My imagination ran riot. I could imagine it being a werewolf. Then I recognised it, it was only next-door's cat!

Oliver Startin (10)
St Wystan's School, Derby

Follow The Path

Larise looked back at Samuel on the path. If they didn't climb the cliff before darkness the lesser dead would have them. They eventually made it only to be attacked by a waffling squiggle. Sam fired a piercing spell and it fried. They were safe for now ...

Philippa Stazicker (10)
St Wystan's School, Derby

The Birds, The Gremlins And The Dragons

The giant, killer birds flew at him from all directions, while gremlins scrambled up the tower. James fended them off best he could, but there were too many of them. Suddenly there was a blood-curdling scream, as the winged beasts flew away while the gremlins fled. The dragons had arrived!

Liam Rhatigan   (10)
St Wystan's School, Derby

Freedom Flight!

Emma and James climbed onto the beast's back.
The winged creature took off into the air
towards the castle. They landed with a soft
crunch in the prisoner's cell. Grasping the
opportunity Mercury leapt onto the creature as
the children slid down. Leaving the ground,
Mercury flew to freedom.

Hollie Strong (10)
St Wystan's School, Derby

The Thing

There was a rustle and a low-pitched growl coming from the bushes. Alexander tried to keep quiet for he knew something was after him. Then there was a loud crash as a tree fell on top of a car. Alexander did what he knew best and fled.

Peter Bralesford (10)

St Wystan's School, Derby

A Missing Dog

We were filming at the hall with a dog called
Charlie. When it was his cue he had vanished. We
searched high and low.
The next day Mandy opened the pantry door and
there was Charlie, guarding Jess the Jack Russell
and her new puppies! The proud father!

Chloe Marshall (10)
St Wystan's School, Derby

The Forest

He stared at the forest in horror, as seven pairs of red eyes stared at us. Tom and I started to walk backwards as we were too scared to run. Seven wolves marched towards us, howled and ran off into the night. They were gone! We were safe for now.

David Boiling (10)
St Wystan's School, Derby

Donna And Her Dream

Donna is having a horrible dream. An alien is in her dream, a terrible alien, a nasty green one. Oh my Lord, it's strangling her, she can't breathe. The alien is a murderer. Donna woke up, 'It was just a dream,' she sighed in relief. Thank the Lord.

Jessica Marshall   (10)
Staveley CE Primary School, Staveley

The Spell That Went Wrong

There's a man called Torara. He's a wizard with a pet called Zuno, a rat. He cast spells on Zuno. One day it went wrong, he cast a spell turning her into a dog. What happened was she turned into a bitch who was nasty with poisoned teeth. She bit him ...

Michaela Raven (11)
Staveley CE Primary School, Staveley

Dragon's Heart

Dragon lay helpless in his hut out beyond the trees. Not one man could see him, he had a heart, no ordinary heart. It was his, he never shared it. Dragon liked to dream, sometimes his dreams were so real only he could believe them. Dragon had one friend.

Charlie Bell (11)

Staveley CE Primary School, Staveley

The Monster Under The Bed

'Tom, it's time for bed,' shouted his mother from
the bottom of the stairs.
'OK,' shouted Tom.
That night Tom suddenly woke up and heard a
strange noise. It seemed to be coming from under
the bed. When he looked he found an Action Man
had fallen from the shelf.

Elizabeth Crawford (11)
Staveley CE Primary School, Staveley

The Sleet Dog

Lauren lived in a girls' orphanage with her best friend, Annie. Laura went to find her parents. Her stepmum was on fire. When she found out Lauren looked up and saw Snow Mount so she started to climb. Then she saw the sleet dog, but he was just a myth.

Tilly Adcock (11)
Staveley CE Primary School, Staveley

Emma's Christmas

Emma entered her room holding her coin, this coin was magic. She looked at her calendar, it was fifty-two days until Christmas. 'I wish it was Christmas every day.' The coin flashed. Emma jumped into bed. When she awoke she found a stocking. 'It's Christmas!'

Frances Butcher (10)
Staveley CE Primary School, Staveley

Shan The Devil

Jack's town was getting attacked by a monstrous devil. Suddenly Jack came with an army, they ran to the town and were starting to attack. They were firing flaming arrows but they made it stronger. Jack then threw water which melted Shan the Devil, but then more came.

Callum Gallop (10)
Staveley CE Primary School, Staveley

Untitled

It's a happy town, everyone believes in the god.
The god Shang is magical, he hears people. The
Devil hated Shang and tried to kill him,
but failed badly.
One day the Devil came down to Earth and almost
killed a human but Shang came down and heard
him.

Andrew Higham (10)
Staveley CE Primary School, Staveley

In The Forest

Slowly Michaela crept into the forest. She had never been there before and she was scared. She walked slowly and silently. Then she heard something and began to run. Suddenly she tripped over a log. There she saw some dragons and unicorns. She stayed thirty seconds then ran home.

Megan Holliday (11)
Staveley CE Primary School, Staveley

The Magic Twig

'What's that?' A blossoming twig. Alice picked it up, took it home, showed Mog (her cat). Mog wished she was a child. The next thing she was!
'Who are you?'
'I'm Mog, I wished to be a child. This twig must be magic. Now I can come to school today!'

Laurie Nuttall (11)
Staveley CE Primary School, Staveley

Viky The Cat

I'm Viky, I'm ginger with green eyes. Yesterday
something terrible happened. I was sitting on my
window when my owner pushed me off and put a
cage there. I looked in, a hamster came out. Sam,
my owner said, 'His name is Shmicel.' Schmicel got
out a gun.

Zoe Higgins (11)
Staveley CE Primary School, Staveley

Magic Mayhem

One day a mystical creature called Dino got loose into the human world. Dino was a fat creature with orange eyes. *I think I'll go and cause mayhem*, he thought. So Dino decided to destroy a small village. He threw his lightning bolts and got into trouble.

Katy Coleman (11)
Staveley CE Primary School, Staveley

Attack!

He crouched hidden in the shadows. Very slowly he turned his head, *twang!* An arrow buried itself inside the wooden beam, inches away from his head. He forced himself to stay calm, he walked forward, another arrow came. He felt it slice into him. He was falling, falling, *crack!*

Christopher Moore (10)
Staveley CE Primary School, Staveley

Mega Morphing Man

Mega Morphing Man went for a walk. He found that there was a wall in his way so he morphed into a hammer and knocked it down. He found it was his morphing machine. His morphing machine pointed at him and fired. He turned into a mirror. The machine disintegrated.

Laurence Bowes (11)
Staveley CE Primary School, Staveley

An Alien

Bang! as a missile fired at my farm. I went out to check to find that my herd of sheep had been taken by an unidentified flying object which shot again in the sky. It left a hole. Now we know that there are such things as aliens.

David-Arthur Opie (11)
Whitemoor CP School, Whitemoor

Untitled

One wintry day, a girl called Britney took her dog out for a walk in the park and on the way she saw a pink and purple rabbit. The dog chased it all the way into the rabbit hole and was never seen again.

Mckenzie Mellow (9)
Whitemoor CP School, Whitemoor

The Newly Born Foal

One stormy night in January there was a palomino
pony that was in foal. She didn't think it would
foal, but to her surprise Fudge had foaled in the
middle of the night and they called the foal,
Starlight.
As the months went by it became a strong
showjumper.

Amy Parkin (11)
Whitemoor CP School, Whitemoor

No More Nightmares

I galloped through the skies that night with three fellow mares, Moonbeam, Comet and Luckystar and the rest of my herd. Down below we saw strange-looking things I'd never seen before called humans. Eclipse the head stallion whinnied so we galloped higher into the sky out of sight.

Millie Macfarlane (11)
Whitemoor CP School, Whitemoor

The Mass Murderer

Once upon a time a man called Freddy was a serial
killer known for many offences including murder,
theft and manslaughter. Jail could not hold him as
they had no evidence against him. Only one woman
could grass him in to the police, but was she
caught?

James Allen (11)
Whitemoor CP School, Whitemoor

Robbery

Once upon a time there was a man who wasn't very nice. He was a robber.
One starry night he sneaked into the Queen's palace, he stole the Crown Jewels. The alarm went off and he jumped out of a window. A policeman put him in jail.

Jamie Hawken (10)
Whitemoor CP School, Whitemoor

Untitled

One night a house was burning. The man who lived in the house saw the ambulance and the fire engine were coming. A boy was trapped in the fire. The fire engine poured water over the fire and the fire was out and the boy was saved.

Scott Walkey (9)
Whitemoor CP School, Whitemoor

The Unhappy Sun

The sun wasn't very happy. He didn't know why, so
he asked his mate, Wind. But Wind didn't know
either. Sun went to see Thunder. He wasn't in.
Poor Sun. On the way home he met Tornado. He
explained why he was glum.
'Wear your hat!' said Tornado.
'Thanks friend.'

Emily Dorson (11)
Whitemoor CP School, Whitemoor

The Dog Disaster

One day a man called Pete and his dog Barker fell off a 195ft cliff. Luckily someone saw him and Barker. They called the coastguard and the air ambulance. He was rescued but his arm was paralysed for life. Unfortunately his dog Barker had lost his sight and one leg.

Charlotte Bloxham (11)
Whitemoor CP School, Whitemoor

Lifeguard

On the sunny beach I was walking around on shells and sand with my sister. We were walking on sand and we went in the sea to play. My sister got stuck out there so I called a lifeguard and he saved her.

Connor Morgan (9)
Whitemoor CP School, Whitemoor

Untitled

One day a boy called Perry went to the park with his mum. At the park Perry played on the bright, shiny slides and the huge red climbing frame. When it was time to go home Perry was really tired. So when he got back home he went to bed.

Perry Toomer (10)
Whitemoor CP School, Whitemoor

The Lost Pony

Suddenly there was a big gust of wind and it travelled through the beautiful lost pony's mane. Her mum had died, her dad abandoned her. It was a dark stormy night and there were hunters about. A hunter caught a glimpse of her and mistook her for a fox. *Bang!*

Melissa Hawkey   (10)
Whitemoor CP School, Whitemoor

The Destroyed Farm

A long, long time ago, there was a farm which was destroyed by a cruel man. All the skinny animals on the farm were sadly killed and all the healthy animals were sold for twenty-four pennies. The farmer moved away and stayed at his beautiful sister's house.

Ellie Simmonds (10)
Whitemoor CP School, Whitemoor

The Kitten

One day I went to a park, there was a little white
kitten. He did not have a collar on. I asked Mum if
we could keep him.
Mum said, 'Yes.'
I took him home and called him Snowy.
After a few weeks he grew into an adult.

Amy McLinden (9)
Whitemoor CP School, Whitemoor

The Naughty Monkey

Once upon a time there was a monkey who liked to eat chocolate. The monkey lived in a Cadbury's factory.

One day the monkey went into the stores and sat on the chocolate pyramid.

A few days later the monkey ate the whole pyramid and he exploded.

Thomas Webber (11)

Whitemoor CP School, Whitemoor

The Mysterious Fish Bowl

Smash! "What was that?' asked Emma. She ran through the house searching for the place where she'd heard the sound. Finally she reached her bedroom. There, Emma found her fish bowl on the floor, smashed. Suddenly, the bowl floated in the air and took Emma to a strange place.

Shannon Toomer (11)
Whitemoor CP School, Whitemoor

A Short Story

Once upon a time Ben's dog Fred ran away and the vigilant police found him in the colossal forest, two miles north, eating a dead bear. Some terrorists shot him and the police. The terrorists lived happily ever after. Or did they?

Callum Dorson (9)
Whitemoor CP School, Whitemoor

Information

We hope you have enjoyed reading this book - and that you will continue to enjoy it in the coming years.

If you like reading and writing, drop us a line or give us a call and we'll send you a free information pack. Alternatively visit our website at **www.youngwriters.co.uk**

Write to:

**Young Writers Information,
Remus House,
Coltsfoot Drive,
Peterborough,
PE2 9JX**

Tel: (01733) 890066